LaRosa Chronicles

Summer
And August

K. Spirito

Published by:
A Snowy Day Distribution & Publishing
P.O. Box 2014
Merrimack, NH 03054

Cover Design: A Snowy Day Distribution & Publishing

First printing: May 2010

ISBN: 978-0-9844681-0-2

Printed in the United States of America

ACKNOWLEDGEMENTS

Chatham, Massachusetts holds a special place in my heart, for it is there, many years ago, I met Eric Linder, owner of Yellow Umbrella Books. Eric was the first on Cape Cod to allow me to do a book signing on the front porch of his eclectic bookshop. Every year since then I have been signing at Yellow Umbrella Books. Eric is one of those unsung heroes we hear about from time to time—on the outside, a solid, quiet visage while on the inside, a heart of gold ready to give the little guy a break. One day Eric asked me why I didn't write a novel set on the Cape. My reply was that I intended to do just that, but when I did, I wanted my work to show how special he, his wife Patty, his employees Karen and Mel, the locals, and the tourists are to me. I cannot thank all of you enough!

Deb Horan of Booklovers' Gourmet, Webster, Massachusetts has also lent rock-solid support to my husband Sal and me throughout the years. Thank you so much, Deb! Her husband, parents, and patrons are some of the sweetest folks I have ever met.

Toadstools Bookshops of Peterborough, Milford, and Keene, New Hampshire, have provided overwhelming support throughout the years. Thank you, Willard Williams, Regina, Brian, Jan, Don, and all!

Sal and I treasure the lasting friendships we have made on Cape Cod throughout the years:

Eric and Patty Linder
Debra Lawless, reporter of the Cape Cod Chronicle
Officer Rodney, CPD
Marty Stiles, member and volunteer of the Cape
Cod Hook Fishermen's Association
The folks at the Cranberry Inn: Bill and Kay
DeFord, Jeff and Lise Wilson, Igor, and Nora.
The breakfast specials were fabulous!
The folks at the Chatham Coffee Company.
Best coffee anywhere!
Stu Sterns—94-years-young!

Sal and I hold dear to our hearts:

Professor Gary Baker of Franklin Pierce University and his lovely wife Sharon.

Peter Lundquist, MD and Nurse Jeanette.

Laurie Alden, Kurt Muhlfelder, Melissa Conway, and all the Franklin Pierce Alumni Association.

New Hampshire Writers' Project.

The wide range of folks who offered me their insights, opinions, experiences, expertise, and critique. I got answers to questions I didn't even think to ask!

All our friends throughout New England, the United States, and around the world!

Special thanks to our Webmaster, computer wiz son, Sal Spirito, Jr. Your technical support is invaluable!
Need website services? visit: www.usshost.com

To my totally bodacious editors: Lisa DiGloria;
Need manuscript editing services? visit: www.bookink.com, Cynthia Godin; Carol Brooks; Deb Horan; Joyce Sunskis—thank you, thank you, thank you!

Thank you, Chris Thompson of Lightning Source.

A million thank yous go out to Eric Linder and Debra Lawless for being vital characters in SUMMER AND AUGUST! I hope I have done you proud!

Most of all, I would be remiss not to point out my husband, children, their spouses, our grandchildren, Mickey Blue Eyes and Ralph. Without all of you, there is no inspiration.

LaRosa Chronicles

Father Sandro's Money (available)

Kathleen (work in progress)

Roses Falling (work in progress)

Time Has A Way (available)

Everything Happens To Margi

(work in progress)

Yesterday, Tommy Gray Drowned (available)

Tomorrow Is Promised To No One

(work in progress)

CANDY-COLORED CLOWN (available)

Spiderling (available)

P I S C A T A G U A (available)

Summer And August (available)

Visit: www.kspirito.com

For Sal:
    Magic Man

JUNE 7 – 9:00 A.M.

MORGUE - CHATHAM, MASSACHUSETTS

"A blow to the back of the head incapacitated Jersey Zayres," Doctor Curt Shirlington said. He hooked his hands onto the pockets of his white lab coat. "At that point, Mr. Zayres either fell or a person—or perhaps persons—all of which are unknown at this time—jostled Mr. Zayres into the dumpster. Impalement through the abdomen by means of a metal corner protector, which had been disposed of during the latest round of renovations at the Chatham Inn and Conference Center, is the ultimate cause of death."

"Impalement," Celia Beale mumbled.

From the opposite side of the stainless steel gurney, Curt noted the manner in which the middle-aged woman, clad in black, scanned the sheet-draped corpse. Her eyes locked on the tag that dangled off the right toe.

FBI Special Agent Robert Pomoroy spoke up, "That's right. Jersey Zayres fell on a metal spike."

Celia Beale slid a sidelong glance at the angular young Fed. Intense eye contact between the two ensued.

Celia Beale remains exceptionally stationary, thought Curt. *Although I did detect a slight furrowing of the brow... She utters nary a word, simply gazes at Robert. Indeed, our Ms. Beale is aware of my young chum directing the investigation of missing drugs at the Rehab Center where she has been employed as a nurse for quite a few years. Jersey Zayres was the fence—that is well known, according to Robert. Be that as it may, the FBI requires hard evidence, he*

1

says. Knowing Robert as I do, I expect that he will stop at nothing to acquire such evidence.

Pomoroy's square jaw hardened, his eyes, camera lenses, photographing every infinitesimal move that Celia Beale made and every infinitesimal emotion. Few agents even came close to achieving the mental and physical acuity that Robert Pomoroy possessed.

Celia Beale blinked—though it was hardly a blink—once. A millisecond later, she broke eye contact and peered down at the corpse. Her bobbed, henna-black hair slopped forward, obscuring a major portion of her face. Her voice materialized in a controlled stammer, "M-murdered?"

Pomoroy snorted. "Certainly appears that way."

Curt scrutinized the brash, bronze-toned Fed who stood a couple of inches taller than the doctor. A navy blue windbreaker, jeans, and white running shoes camouflaged a lean, muscular, six-foot frame. *Ah, yes,* Curt reflected. *I do recall a time of being that vibrant, that brazen. Indeed, youth is wasted on the young.*

"My poor, poor Jersey."

Celia Beale's moaning hauled Curt out of deepening retrospection. His shoulder twitched, triggering him into noticing her hands that were cupping the lifeless cheeks of Jersey Zayres. *Don't tell me the woman is about to make a spectacle of herself by kissing the deceased.* However, Celia Beale did not kiss the lifeless cheeks of Jersey Zayres. Instead, she let go and straightened. Cocking her head to one side, she just looked at the corpse, her face unreadable. A moment passed. Her hand patted the naked left shoulder and then began to drift, down the naked bicep, down to elbow, down beneath the sheet that mounded as if a serpent slithering all but undetected by an intended prey.

Curt clasped his hands, struggling to contain outrage. *Such action borders on the perverse!*

The sheet flattened somewhat as her fingers spread out, bridging the lifeless hand of Jersey Zayres. Once again, the sheet mounded as she clutched his hand then towed it out into the open. She bent to kiss it, but paused, her eyes narrowing upon the band of pale skin at the base of the hand's third finger. "Ring... Where is Jersey's diamond ring? He always wears that diamond ring." Her eyes darted to the dead man's ear. "And his diamond earring... Jersey always wears that, too."

"Take it easy, Ma." Anxiety clouded the face of twenty-one-year-old Quincy Beale as he rubbed her shoulder.

So that is it, thought Curt, analyzing Celia and Quincy Beale. *Jersey Zayres sought the good life via illicit drug trafficking on Cape Cod, perhaps intending to make it big so that at some point in the future, he might retire to South Florida to run a fishing charter business. Ah, yes, our dear Celia Beale—and perchance the innocent-appearing Quincy—had it in mind to hitch a ride on Mr. Zayres' upward mobility.*

Celia Beale appeared taller now, having stiffened her pear-shaped five-foot-two frame. No longer was she clutching the lifeless hand. Instead, both of her hands were clamped onto her hipbones. Her black eyes, sharper than a surgeon's scalpel, were dissecting Quincy. His entire being wilted. Her gaze shifted to the head of the gurney, riveting on Detective Rodney Clement of the Chatham Police Department. Hostility grated her voice. "What about Jersey's wallet? I suppose that is also missing? Who found my Jersey in that nasty dumpster anyways? And where's his clothes? What happened to all his stuff?"

Clement appeared unruffled, although splotches of red were beginning to pepper his face. "We are holding Mr. Zayres' effects until the conclusion of the case."

"Conclusion of the case," echoed Celia Beale, her voice half an octave higher than before. Her right hand yanked back her hair as she zeroed in for a better view of the detective. Her gypsy eyebrows arched.

"Yes, ma'am." Clement gave a casual nod. "At the conclusion of the case, Mr. Zayres' effects will be released to next of kin."

"Jersey didn't have relatives!" spewed Celia Beale. She puffed up her chest and jounced her hands. "And you know what? Jersey was going to marry me!" She wide eyed Quincy, nodding at him. "Isn't that right, honey?"

The young man shifted uncomfortably, his sunken eyes avoiding hers. "Yeah, Ma."

Celia Beale pursed her lips. Hooking her hands on her hips once again, she sent the detective a full-bodied so-there nod.

Clement's ruddy brow tightened.

So much for detached professionalism, Curt thought. *Indeed, this situation is becoming volatile.* He cleared his throat—loudly—the way his English-born father always did when as a youngster, Curt had erred—and gestured toward the exit. "Shall we continue this discussion in the medical examiner's office? Detective Clement, will you be so kind as to direct the way?"

As Curt leaned over to draw the sheet up over the head of the corpse, he noticed Quincy Beale take Celia Beale's arm. However, Celia Beale remained steadfast. Curt could hear her teeth grinding.

Quincy Beale gave a light tug. Celia Beale squinted at his hand and then up at his tormented face. What meager color the young man possessed drained swifter than water in a low-flush toilet. His hand fell away. Her eyes shot back to the sheet-draped corpse, thinning to mere slits. "Pearle did it," she hissed.

Quincy stumbled backward. "Ma! Don't say that!"

Curt exchanged silent astonishment with Pomoroy. They glanced at Clement who was staring back at them, red splotches swarming his face and neck. "Pearle?" mumbled the detective.

Struggling to appear unruffled, Clement fished a stub of a pencil and a crinkled spiral pad out of his shirt pocket, "Who is this Pearle?"

Celia Beale ignored the question, focusing instead on Quincy who was now a light shade of green. The young man appeared to be on the verge of vomiting. In a low rumbling seethe, she insisted, "Pearle did it, honey. You and I both know it was Pearle who murdered our dear Jersey."

His hands covered his ears as Quincy waved his head side-to-side, cowering so much that his five-feet-nine stature seemed cut in half.

Clement tapped the pencil on the pad, managing to portray a fair amount of indignation. "Ms. Beale. I must have the last name of this Pearle individual you keep talking about."

Celia Beale glared at the detective. "Key! Pearle Key! Yes, that Pearle was so horribly jealous of Jersey and me! That's how come she murdered my Jersey! And I bet I was going to be next!"

"Ma, please..." Moisture glazed Quincy Beale's eyes. "You can't mean that."

Celia Beale broke into a crying jag. "But she did, honey!" Celia Beale threw herself across the sheet-draped corpse. "Jersey was going to marry me! And...and Pearle didn't like it at all and so she murdered him! Pearle murdered my poor, poor Jersey!"

Summer And August

JUNE 6 - 3 P.M.

CHATHAM INN AND CONFERENCE CENTER

Eighteen hours earlier, Hank Night itched the left side of his scruffy chin with his jagged, filth-imbedded fingernails while eyeballing empty soda cans and plastic cups, dirty paper plates and crumpled napkins, place cards and seminar evaluation forms that littered the tables and floor like late-autumn leaves discarded by the trees that bore them. Blue metal folding chairs were askew; one chair was actually overturned. A scant few were folded up and braced against tables. None of this helped the drug and alcohol hangover from which the janitor was suffering. Speaking the lingo of the street, he carped, "Hafta score heavy-duty stuff after clearin' out this pigsty, that's for sure. Alky and funny cigs jes' ain't gonna cut it this time."

"I say, you are indeed a wet blanket," blustered Doctor Curt Shirlington, laying a hand on Hank Night's shoulder. The two men were about the same height; however, that was the only resemblance. The easy-going, fortyish doctor with an English-Scottish accent was impeccably groomed, wearing a blue-striped button-down shirt, navy blue tie that matched his sport coat and pants, and black loafers. The janitor, on the other hand, found life nothing more than a hassle and his failure to deal with it accounted for his unkempt and pasty appearance. How long he had lived on the streets was anybody's guess. The homeless man could not be bothered with showering, shaving, or combing his scraggly gray hair; and he refused to wash his clothes. On the rare occasion that he felt the need for clean clothes, he either begged for some at a local church bazaar or stole some off a clothesline. *Easiest is from the unlocked cars. Thank the devil for tourists*, Hank always said.

His black eyes leered at the hand on his shoulder. "Wet blanket," Hank muttered. He squinted at the blue-eyed doctor. "That remark's welcome as crotch rot."

"Oh," Curt blustered. "Do pardon me."

The janitor pursed his lips, twisting them up one side of his face. He pulled away and shambled to the nearest table where his gnarly fingers snagged the corners of the tablecloth. "Busted my stones makin' everythin' just so. Aye-yup, just so. I know, 'cause I was the one who done it. And now look. Some pea-brained la-di-dah even went so far as to gnaw up napkins and huck spitballs all over the place." His head throbbed as he drew the corners of the tablecloth together and in the process, overturned a Styrofoam cup that was half-full of stale coffee. "Now, will ya look at that..." As the curdled liquid spattered the floor, Hank shook his head and it made him nauseous. "Like I got time for this crap."

The doctor let out a boisterous laugh and it struck the janitor like a lightning bolt. About to give Doctor Curt Shirlington a piece of his mind, Hank heard, "You coming, Curt?" A one-eyed leer over the shoulder immediately consumed the homeless man in festering loathing because standing between the open French doors that led to the front portico was a tall great-pretender who just happened to resemble that smart-aleck model on the tanning oil poster plastered to the window of the Ben Franklin Store. "Now ain't you sweet?" Hank sneered under his breath. The left side of his upper lip twitched. "Life sure is good now ain't it, pretty boy?"

"Run along, Robert," Curt called out. "I will be along shortly."

The janitor glanced at the doctor who was loosening his tie. "Now what're you up to?"

Curt pulled the tie out of his shirt collar then rolled it up and stuffed it into the pocket of his sport coat. "I am going to lend you a hand, my good fellow." He removed his sport coat and hooked it over a chair.

"Goody two-shoes," Hank sniped, eyes rolling. He crushed the coffee-soaked tablecloth into a papery snowball then stuffed it into the blue duck cloth cart. He set about clearing the rest of the tables in the same manner, a process that should have taken about fifteen minutes, but usually took him about an hour. Doing so maximized puny wages, which at times, forced the homeless man on off days to bum all the way to Hyannis and hop the train for Sandwich to spend a day or two meandering among the shrubbery of tidy backyards, seeking unlocked backdoors. Between six and seven in the evening was the best time to score—that was the time when summer people took off for supper at the Daniel Webster Inn or other inns and restaurants that were within easy walking distance. Most hot summer nights, he spent mooching *cool z's* behind the gristmill. *Sure was peaceful there, what with that waterfall and all.* Catching the train back to the elbow of the Cape, he mooched a few more *cool z's* on top of the baggage car and felt refreshed upon jumping off, ready to pedal purloined wares to unscrupulous drug dealers or unsuspecting tourists. *Thank the devil for tourists.*

Hank eyeballed the door that led to the loading dock. He was still stinging from an earlier confrontation near the dumpster. *Drugs used to be easier to get than alcohol. That second-rate drug dealer Zayres sure is getting real stingy lately. Too garl-darn overcautious, that Jersey.* The homeless man scratched the left side of his neck, craving a hit—any kind of hit. *Then again, what with the law cracking down on drug related crimes on the Cape...* He ran his hand along his shoulder to release tension. *Claims he's connected to the mob. Now ain't that a broken record, Jersey, my man?* Hank snorted. *Well now, if that's true, no heat's gonna pester you. Nope. No way, Jersey. Don't believe it for one pissy-smelling Port-a-Potty minute. Everybody knows the mob's got the fuzz in its pockets.*

The janitor straightened, sucking in air to fend off nausea. *Stinkin' Jersey Zayres. Why's he hafta up the price again? Try and rip me off, will ya?*

Hank made a couple of clicking noises. *Problem is: I'm in such a desperate need for a hit—now more than ever, what with havin' ta clear out this pigsty. A hit of any kind'll do. Any kind. That's all I need. Even if it ends up bein' that low-quality poison smart-mouth Jersey hawks. Mob don't vend low quality junk like that. Makes me sick as a dog. But it does the trick. I get so high I swear I can hear the angels sing.* The janitor laced his forearms through a couple of folded chairs and headed to get the chair rack, which was inside the storage closet on the other side of the door—the door that led to the loading dock...and the dumpster. *Aye-yup, high enough to hear the angels sing.*

By the time Hank returned to the conference room, Doctor Shirlington was looking quite disgruntled, leaning his weight against the trash cart. "I say, ol' chap, collection is at last complete. Be that as it may, I must assure you that I had no intentions of cleaning the entire facility when I first agreed to lend a hand."

The janitor winced. "S-sorry, Doc." He latched onto the cart and tramped once again toward the rear door. He heard Curt let out a huff and then tag along, dragging a trash barrel—the one with wheels that squealed like a stuck pig. The racket nearly drowned out the do-gooder.

"All that's left, my good man, is a final sweep and mopping."

"Is that all," scoffed the janitor, ramming the cart into the door. On the other side, an ugly purple sky darkened the loading dock like midnight. Thunder was grumbling in the distance.

"Say goodbye to the sun, my good man," said Curt.

The homeless man grunted. "Good riddance." He plodded to the dumpster at the far end of the dock and upended the cart. He grunted some more then backed away and spat off to the side of the dumpster. He stepped over to the doctor and seized the barrel. Maintaining a grip, he tipped the mouth of the barrel toward the dumpster. A quick jerk backward and the contents puked out. "Like a drunk on Saturday night." He sniggered. "Sure know what that's like." He did an about face and in the midst of taking a footstep, stopped, eyes narrowing. His head rolled over his shoulder and then his face contracted like a prune.

"I say, upon what are you deliberating?" asked Curt.

Hank scratched the back of his head while eyeing the putrid refuse beset with deerflies, greenheads, plus every other form of creepy-crawly known to humanity—or so it seemed to the homeless man. "Somethin' ain't kosher, Doc." His head throbbed as out of the corner of his eye, he noticed Curt rotating toward the dumpster, thumb and index finger tugging at a clean-shaven chin.

"Sorry, ol' chap. You do have me at a loss."

The janitor clenched and unclenched his hands, straining not to puke. "Somethin' just ain't right. No way, no how." His eyes skimmed the alley and then the loading dock. "How 'bout a look-see?"

"Look-see?" echoed Curt.

Hank coughed up a blob of sour-tasting phlegm and hucked it at the side of the dumpster. He watched it ooze down the green metal for a long moment. It should have made him feel better to be rid of it. He jammed his hands into his hips and looked around. "Nothin' better than a garl-darn push broom?"

"Push broom?" echoed the doctor.

Heaving an all-consuming sigh, the janitor stepped to the push broom. With an arcing swing of the arm, he snatched it up. He rolled the brush end this way then back again, studying the edges. Doing so aggravated his unstable condition. "This oughter get her done."

"Get what done?"

"Weight of this here brush'll yank me smack into that there swill if I ain't careful about it." Hank choked back his belly as he eyed the stick end. "Hmm." Holding the broom like a divining rod, he swung the brush end back and forth.

"I say, ol' chap, I am completely at wit's end."

The janitor gave a self-satisfied nod. "Aye-yup." He grinned, a yellow tartar grin, at the do-gooder then stepped to the dumpster and probed the layers of trash.

Curt leaned in close. "Is that a leather wingtip shoe I see?"

Hank bug eyed the highly polished black leather. "Well, I'll be a spanked baby's butt."

Curt pointed. "Nudge aside a layer or two of that trash right there."

"Whatever you say, Doc."

"A leg is connected to that wingtip!" spouted Curt. "Wait a minute! I see a hand! Stop!"

Hank felt the doctor's fingertips dig into his bicep, tugging him backward.

"Best not disturb one bit more," said Curt. "It would appear that an individual has been run through with a metal spike of some sort. Such a discovery behooves the summoning of gendarmes."

A shiver raced through the homeless man. "Whatever, uh, you say…Doc." When the doctor released his arm, Hank felt an eerie sense of relief wash over him.

Curt whipped a cell phone out of his pocket, hit the speed dial, and put the phone to his ear. Waiting for a response on the other end, he met Hank's gaze. "I say, my good fellow, do you have knowledge as to whose remains are among the refuse?"

The janitor blinked. *Remains?* He broke eye contact and gulped. "Seen the guy around some," he stammered. At any moment, his head was going to explode. "Heard someone say his name once. Think it's Jersey."

"And his first name?"

"Uhm…I think Jersey's his first name."

Curt suddenly straightened. "Doctor Shirlington here. I am situated behind the Chatham Inn and Conference Center on Shore Road. The body of a deceased male has turned up in the dumpster. Name is Jersey… Hold on." He let the phone sag onto his shoulder while focusing in on the janitor. "Jersey who?"

"Lemme think a minute, Doc." Avoiding eye contact, the homeless man looked up and that was when raindrops spattered his face. "Aargh! Hate water worse than spiders!" He rammed the push broom against the outside frame of the dumpster and sought shelter beneath the meager canopy shielding the backdoor of the Conference Center.

"I say, Hank, the bloke's last name is imperative!"

Queasiness washed over the janitor.

"My good man! Time is of the essence, what with the onset of that squall! Last name, if you will!"

"Zayres!" belched Hank. He jammed his fist against his lips to fend off nausea.

Curt put the phone to his ear once again. "The name is Jersey Zayres. Please send investigators ASAP."

Hank eyeballed the exposed body parts. Spasms tweaked his left eyelid. He dropped his fist from his mouth and spat off to the side of the loading dock. "Ain't given much thought to dying, but that ain't no way I'm intendin' to go down the glory road."

Lightning zigzagged across the brutal sky; an instant later, a thunderclap loud enough to make eardrums bleed. Chatham quaked. The homeless man covered his head with his hands. "I'm outta here!" As he fled down the stairs, rain pelted the loading dock.

The push broom began to slip. As Hank Night disappeared into the squall that swathed the parking lot, the push broom toppled into the dumpster and landed with a double thwack upon the corpse that was pinned by a metal corner protector to the trash. Jersey Zayres, the lowest form of trash.

JUNE 6 – 10 P.M.

THE SHIRLINGTON RESIDENCE

"I see the majority of our guests have taken their leave," said Curt, hanging up his rain-soaked sport coat on the antique wooden coat rack inside the front door. He was relieved to be home—home, a hundred-year-old white manor that had been built by a sea captain. Located on Honeysuckle Lane, off Stage Harbor Road, the neighborhood was an eclectic blend of residents—fishermen, retirees, summer people, and tourists—two miles south of the Chatham Inn and Conference Center, a mile south of the Medical Examiner's Office and Morgue located in the Chatham Police Department on Depot Road, and an easy walk to his office on Cross Street. Nearby, a short trail scented by rosa rugosa led to Old Ice House Pond where water birds moved quietly wiling away the day. To the right was a white cedar swamp—most of which belonged to the town of Chatham—and more trails. The pond emptied into Stage Harbor making it possible for Curt to take an easy row—gunk holing, as Cape Codders so aptly put it—and marvel at the colors of the water changing with the sunrise—or the sunset as the case might be—while fish pocked the surface and seabirds dived. At night, the white light of Stage Harbor Lighthouse seemed to choreograph the glint of channel markers, buoys, and passing watercraft. The area provided summer solace and heat relief.

Many of the old-style Cape Cod structures had been bought, torn down, and replaced with lavish vacation homes, devastating the ecological balance. Recently, Curt and Penny Shirlington joined the movement to preserve that which was left. *The ecological balance of my life, it would seem, is verging on devastation,* mused Curt as he ran his hands through his grimy hair.

He trudged into the dining room where his wife Penny was sitting at the oak table, her hands enfolding a flowery teacup. Although the evening meal had been cleared for several hours, a faint odor of garlic bread lingered in the air. He leaned over and kissed her.

"You missed Janice and Adam by an hour," she said. "Katrina and Casey took off right after dinner. For some reason, they had to get back to New Hampshire."

"For some reason," muttered Robert Pomoroy, who was sitting across the table from Penny.

Curt straightened and gave a nod to the young man. "Robert."

Pomoroy saluted with a bottle of Cape Cod IPA Beer. "Doc."

"Long day, 'ey, old man?"

"You might say that," said Pomoroy. He took a swig of beer.

Curt sent the FBI agent a furtive glance. He had known the young man long enough to recognize he was still stinging from losing Katrina Waters to Casey Hiller. Well aware of how that felt, Curt reflected: *Over the years, I have come to realize that a bloke is not always given what he thinks he wants. He is given what he needs, which includes people who help him, people who hurt and leave him, people who love him and are meant to be the ones who stay close to him and make him into what he is meant to be. I dare say Robert needs an elegant, strong damsel like Penny. It is my fervent hope that one will come along soon. However, the next hurdle will be for that damsel to successfully refocus our dear Robert's eye off Katrina Waters.*

"Are you hungry?" asked Penny, endeavoring to pry her pregnant form off the chair.

Curt gently pressed on her shoulder. "A bit later, my dear wife. It would appear that I have gone beyond the hunger stage."

She smiled up at him. From the look of her, she was entirely satisfied to remain seated.

Guilt washed over him. "I do so apologize. I should have been here, giving you a hand…"

She patted his hand. "Don't worry about it. We both agreed that you should take the post as temporary medical examiner slash coroner."

"Ah, yes, but a murder in Chatham was the farthest thing from our minds."

"Hindsight is twenty-twenty," she said.

"Indeed," said Curt, heading for the bar. "Truly unfortunate that my predecessor has decided to take early retirement. It would seem that the diagnosis of colon cancer prompted him to take a step back and enjoy this earthly life."

Pomoroy spoke up, "It's too bad a replacement hasn't been found. After all, taking a step back and enjoying life was the reason you and Penny quit the CDC and came to Cape Cod in the first place."

"A truly unfortunate state of affairs," said Curt, mixing a Rob Roy in an old-fashion glass. "That it is." He reflected on his consumption of alcohol: *It has diminished since leaving the CDC—drastically since Penny and I relocated to Chatham and established our practice. On the other hand, discovering a cadaver in the dumpster has proven extremely stressful this day; a situation which calls for something somewhat stronger than mere tea to successfully dull the edge. Peace of mind is indeed elusive.*

"I took a walk to Yellow Umbrella Books this afternoon," said Penny. "Eric helped me pick out a book on genealogy."

Curt chuckled, aware that Penny intuitively perceived his stress and was skirting talk of the apparent murder—and the possibility that the position of medical examiner was going to last a lot longer than a mere short term. "You insist that there is more to our family tree than meets the eye," he said.

She shrugged. "You never know. Janice told me that after Emma LaRosa passed on, facts about her side of the family came out that nobody ever knew about. And you know, it wasn't too long ago that unmarried pregnant girls were sent away so as not to shame their families. Their babies were given up for adoption without any records of parenthood."

"So many circumstances can cloud one's background," said Curt. He took a substantial swallow of Rob Roy then smacked his lips.

"Exactly," said Penny. "Who knows where you and I really fit in the scheme of things."

"Perplexing to be at the end of one's family tree," said Curt, rolling the old-fashion glass between his hands. "Brings to mind the subject Katrina spoke of at the seminar today. Abducted children. Many—if they survive the abduction—never uncover their origins."

Penny frowned. "It's so frustrating that Janice and Adam's twins were never found. You can tell by their faces they have never let it go."

Sipping his drink, Curt pondered the abduction of four-year-old fraternal twins, Summer and August LaRosa, born to Janice and Adam LaRosa. *It has been a number of years since it happened. At least fifteen. Can't be twenty though. Before the Amber Alert System could have lent some assistance. It was a time when missing children stayed*

18

missing—as in the case of Summer and August LaRosa. These days, sexual predators brazenly discard young bodies intending them to be found, thereby making names for themselves—albeit despicable names, which, of course, means nothing in the end, the intention of those dastardly predators being everlasting notoriety.

"Terrible headlines," said Penny. She shivered. "And the abduction happened right there on the busy streets of Brighton, Massachusetts, yet nobody saw or heard one blessed thing."

"Back then," said Pomoroy, without looking up, "it cost too much to mail photographs and descriptions to every police and sheriff station in the country. Computers do that now, though there is some cost in doing that, too. But in the case of the LaRosa twins, the trail has gone so cold that municipal budgets deter any further investigation. So what happened to those kids is anybody's guess. Come to think of it, I've never seen an age-progression image of them. Do you know if any have been done?"

"I am not aware of any," said Curt, "but knowing Adam and Janice as I do, I am sure they have done that."

"They have," said Penny. "Several times. I saw some a couple of years ago."

"I'd like to take a look at those images," said Pomoroy.

"I'll ask Janice for one the next time I talk to her," said Penny. "But you know, they sure were lucky the kidnapper—or kidnappers—didn't take Eliot, too."

Thinking out loud, Curt said, "At first, authorities suspected Janice's first husband."

"It was no secret he resented her and Eliot for being so happy with Adam," said Penny. "Can you imagine? *His own son wanted* to be adopted by another man! How do you think the guy felt about that?"

Curt drew back the side of his face, waving his head side-to-side. "The adoption took quite a while, as I recall."

"So the theory that the ex kidnapped the twins didn't pan out," said Pomoroy.

"That's because authorities found him locked up in a Mexican jail," said Penny, "for beating up a woman who—get this!—was pregnant with his child!"

"The bloke had been in Mexico for quite some time," said Curt, "incarcerated in that jail for over a month prior to the kidnapping."

"If a bright cloud exists at all in such a tragedy," said Penny, "is that Eliot was away, visiting a cousin in Stoneham when the abduction of Summer and August took place."

"My belief has always been that the kidnapper..." said Curt.

"Or kidnappers," added Penny.

Curt nodded. "They planned the deed to coincide with Janice going into the hospital to have her fourth child."

"Autumn," said Penny, dreamily. "Don't you just love the names Janice and Adam came up with? Summer, August, Autumn."

Pomoroy rolled his eyes. "Don't let Eliot hear you say that."

"And what, my dear wife," Curt said, "is amiss with the name we have chosen for our child?"

Her eyelashes fluttered at Curt while putting the flowery ceramic teacup to her lips. Several moments passed. Setting down the cup on the saucer, she said, "Katrina insists those twins have got to be somewhere. She says somebody has them locked up somewhere and they can't get home. That girl is so bent on tracking down those twins."

"And the wee one just might succeed," said Curt. "I say, she did an indubitably fine job at the seminar today."

He glanced at Pomoroy and instantly regretted that the subject of Katrina had once again arisen. He chugged down the last of the Rob Roy then mixed another one and headed for the captain's chair at the head of the table. On the way, he tapped the young man on the shoulder.

Pomoroy swilled down the last of the beer and set the empty bottle on the table—a little harder than he should have. "So who's the dumpster stiff?"

Penny glared at the young Fed. "Just had to go and open that can of worms, didn't you?"

Curt lowered himself onto the chair. "Ah, my dear wife, you try so hard to protect my psychological well-being."

Her face flushed. "Well, somebody has to," she grumbled, squinting into her empty teacup.

Curt cupped his hand over hers.

She looked up at him.

He winked.

She smiled.

He smiled back.

Pomoroy harrumphed and shoved back his chair. He got to his feet then trudged off to the kitchen.

Penny and Curt heard the refrigerator door open and the clink of bottles. "Robert should just move in with us," she said. "He's here all the time anyways."

"The hearty breakfast specials at the Cranberry Inn keep him there," Curt said.

Penny drew up the side of her face. "Yeah, breakfast around here is hit or miss."

"His accommodations next to the lobby afford easy access in his line of business," Curt said.

On the way back, with a bottle of Cape Cod beer in his hand, Pomoroy stopped at the doorframe and leaned against it. He took a swig of the brew then said, "With that wicked thunderstorm that barreled in, crime scene investigators must've had one heck of a time shielding evidence."

"Aye," said Curt, toying with Penny's wedding band. "Several inn workers and I pitched in; albeit, the entire canopy was nearly lost—ourselves included—to the gale. The lightning was horrendous."

Pomoroy took a slug of beer. "Scared the bejesus out of you, I'll bet."

"To say the least," said Curt. "Nevertheless, to answer your question, Robert, the janitor, a Mister Hank Night, identified the *stiff*—as you so aptly put it, Robert—as Jersey Zayres."

Pomoroy's eyebrows shot to his hairline. "No kidding!"

"You knew him," stated Curt.

"I knew him," said Pomoroy.

Curt squinted at the young Fed who was returning to the table.

"Jersey Zayres was an upstart hawk in Chatham's drug trafficking," said Pomoroy. "He did away with the previous fence. FBI can't prove it. Nope. The carcass hasn't turned up."

"Yet," added Curt.

"Yet," echoed Pomoroy, a slow smirk buttered his face.

"So Jersey Zayres was bracing to take over the entire drug trade on Cape Cod," said Curt.

"Stepping on lots of toes," added Pomoroy. "I figured all along Zayres' days were numbered. Still, I wish I had more time to track his activities."

"So that's why you've been hanging around Chatham," said Penny. "I was getting worried that you were onto some kind of terrorist activity."

A slow smirk lifted Pomoroy's lips. "Sometimes the biggest prizes are under the smallest pebbles."

22

"Indeed," said Curt. He took several pensive sips of his Rob Roy, which emptied the glass. He glanced up at Pomoroy. "As with Penny and me, you came to Cape Cod more to escape terrorism than to look for it."

Pomoroy winced. "That's a fact. Terrorism interrupted my life at a very young age—just as it did..."

Aware that Pomoroy had stopped short of saying Katrina's name, Curt and Penny exchanged glances. Moments passed. Penny spoke up, "Nailing drug dealers instead of terrorists must feel like a bit of heaven, Robert."

Pomoroy rolled his eyes. "I wouldn't say that."

Again, moments passed. This time, Curt spoke up, "Has your investigation proven fruitful?"

The young Fed heaved a chest full of air. "Jersey Zayres was small potatoes. Scum like him can be taken down like that." Pomoroy snapped his fingers. "What I want is the suppliers—cut drug trafficking off right at the source. Too bad Zayres went and got himself knocked off. Sure would have loved to nail those suppliers."

"Regretfully, I have a sense that the crime has not yet reached its conclusion," said Curt.

"Jersey," mumbled Penny, suddenly consumed in thought. "I heard that name before... Yes! At the Rehab Center! I was there for the meeting a while back. Remember? It was about the new computer system."

"That system has certainly turned into a bit of a boondoggle," said Curt. "Lately, processing patient information at the Rehab Center had been a hassle to say the least."

"Screwed up my investigation, that's for sure," said Pomoroy.

Penny rolled her eyes while nodding in agreement. "Anyways, I overheard one of the nurses from oncology talking to another one about the new love in her life—a guy named Jersey something-or-other. The first name caught

23

my ear: Jersey—what an odd name, I thought. Sounded gangster-ish. Funny thing: when I looked over at that nurse, I did a double take at her hair. It was blacker than ink. The other nurse's was muddy brown. The two of them use way too much henna."

"I didn't know women used henna these days," said Curt.

"It's used more than you know," said Pomoroy. "I don't have to remind you of Regina Waters, do I?"

Curt winced. *Now there was a woman everyone loved to hate,* he thought.

Pomoroy peered sideways at Penny. "Do you recall the nurse's name?"

"Gosh, I don't know." Penny seemed to shut down while wracking her brain. After several moments, her face brightened. "But I can find out!" She yanked her cell phone out of her pocket then hunted through her contact list. She hit send. "Hey, Ann. Say, you know those two oncology nurses with the henna hair? Yeah, that's them! Remember the one who says she's going out with a guy named Jersey? Huh? What was that? The one who skunks up the wards with all that cheap perfume she pours on herself?" Penny giggled, holding her pregnant belly with her free hand. "That's way too funny! So what's her name? Okay, thanks. Talk to you later." Penny flipped the cell phone off and gave an amused nod.

"Don't tell me," said Pomoroy. "Henna head is Celia Beale."

JUNE 7 - 7:30 A.M.

THE KEY RESIDENCE

"Don't tell me the perves got another one," sputtered Beverly Key when an Amber Alert flashed across the screen of her computer. Sitting at the desk beside the window in the far corner of the living room, the twenty-one-year-old wrapped a wayward strand of her shoulder length, henna-enhanced brunette hair around her ear. Her childlike sapphire eyes scanned the breaking news:

> Boston, Massachusetts. Authorities are searching for nine-year-old Stephanie Marie Violetta believed to have been abducted by a person or persons unknown at this time. Parents reported Stephanie missing when she didn't return after taking the daily trash out of their home located in East Boston. Police say several teenagers in the area witnessed a maroon Ford sedan speeding away twenty minutes prior to the parents reporting Stephanie missing. The driver of the maroon Ford was a white male in his late 30s or early 40s. Stephanie Marie Violetta is Caucasian with brown eyes and hair, 4 feet 2 inches tall and weighing 55 pounds.

Beverly took in air and it felt as if she hadn't drawn a breath in minutes. Her slender tan fingers were frozen on the keyboard and when she took them away, they were stiff; her entire slender five-foot-five frame was stiff. Flexing her fingers, she slumped against the back of the chair. "Doesn't seem as though these alerts are curtailing this stuff at all. If anything, it seems to be giving the sickos even more publicity."

The muffled sound of tires on crushed shells drew her attention to the window. It was closed; however earlier, she had pushed aside the bottom tiers of the white café curtains to allow the early morning sunshine to warm up the living room. "Good, Mom's home." She straightened and looked out at the driveway. Disappointment struck. It wasn't Pearle Key's black Saab. Although it was a black car—entering the driveway next door.

The Key and Beale two-bedroom cottages, which were the last two structures on the dead end Easy Street in North Chatham, were mirror images of each other. Like many other homes on the Cape, their wood siding possessed a weathered gray appearance. Sea roses and blue hydrangea added color to the two modest yards that were defined by white picket fences in the front and sides. The Atlantic Ocean lapped the far end of the backyards. A gate between the parallel driveways provided quick access between the two properties. Needless to say, the two families were close, real close. Rumor had it that Pearle Key and Celia Beale were gay. However, that wasn't all that unusual or any big deal to Beverly—or Quincy, for that matter—given the gay community on Cape Cod. It was just a part of every-day life, they figured—the likely reason neither one found the rumors embarrassing. *Heck, on any given night, tourists flock to Provincetown to take in the street life that brings traffic to a standstill. And so what if Mom and Aunt Celia are gay? They managed to survive without husbands. My rotten excuse for a father ran off— before I was even born. Quincy was three years old when his father took off. Funny how Aunt Celia goes out of her way to make Quincy look different from his father—whatever he looked like. She says she always had a thing for blond surfer types, so she makes sure Quincy fits the image—all the way to bleaching his hair. Thank goodness, she's not into green or blue or some other weird hair color. Sometimes, I don't know how Quincy puts up with Aunt Celia. Then again, nobody goes against Aunt Celia—not even Mom.*

A second car entered the driveway next door. It was white with a dark blue stripe outlined in orange running horizontally along the side and across the trunk to the other side. White letters within the blue stripe identified the vehicle: Chatham Police.

Tongue in cheek, Beverly quipped, "What have you done now, Quincy?"

All through high school, Quincy had been the class clown, always showing off. *Oh, how his chocolate eyes twinkled whenever he pulled off some sort of dumb prank. He always managed to charm his way out of a jam. I'll never forget the time he ate a beetle—of course, it wasn't a real beetle, which I found out later. Some difference when he's around Aunt Celia—a real Mama's boy. "Yes, Ma. Of course, Ma." I really think he's going to college just to get away from her. Things are so different now that we're in college— different colleges. Something's missing between him and me. Not only that he's going for marine exploration in Woods Hole and I'm taking law enforcement in Sandwich. Don't know what direction law enforcement will take me—awful lot of weird stuff going on these days.*

So as it was, the Keys and Beales were closer than most neighbors. Celia and Pearle had traded off babysitting so each could work different shifts as oncology nurses at the Rehab Center. After paying the monthly mortgages, they scraped funds together for clothing, household needs, and entertainment that consisted mostly of things that required little money—such as the times the two women took the children down to the Chatham Dock on Stage Harbor Road and begged a local fisherman to borrow his whaler so that they could row out to Monomoy Island for a picnic. On the way to the island, Beverly and Quincy squealed with delight at the countless seals bobbing their heads in the glistening sea. "Aunt Celia is so lucky," murmured Beverly. "She has her own boat now. Jersey gave it to her. Funny how Aunt Celia swore Mom and me and Quincy to secrecy about it. And you'd think she'd invite Mom and me to go with them to Monomoy by now. I suppose she never will as long as Jersey's around. But I sure miss our picnics, Quincy."

When Beverly and Quincy turned sixteen, Pearle and Celia managed to scrounge up enough money to buy the fledgling drivers wheels: a faded red VW Bug for Beverly and a rickety blue Nissan pickup for Quincy. It was a miracle either vehicle ran at all. Beverly always knew when Quincy was coming or going, mostly because the crunch of his tires was heavier than most. Plus, there was no mistaking the rumble of the engine. One way or the other, she always looked out her bedroom window whenever he came or went. *Quincy used to always look up at me, smile, wave. Now, he acts like this house doesn't even exist—like Mom and I don't exist.* Beverly drew in a breath, longing to reconnect. *Yes, things were tight, but we were still a regular family until...well...until that Jersey Zayres came along six months ago. And then things really cooled off when he moved in with Aunt Celia a month ago. Quincy can't stand that jerk at all.*

Beverly braced her left elbow on the desk and rested her chin in the palm of her hand. She barely acknowledged the driver getting out of the unmarked car, which was now parked behind Quincy's truck and Celia's black Saab. The driver's manner of dress—brown sport coat, trousers, and shoes, yellow shirt, and brown striped tie—led her to assume that he was a plainclothes detective. A younger man got out of the passenger-side door. He was wearing a blue windbreaker, jeans, and white running shoes. *Must be another detective.* She straightened, watching the two men walk beneath the white archway into the tidy yard. Then two uniformed officers got out of the black and white. All four were scanning the area like coyotes on the lookout for prey. The man in the sport coat rang the doorbell. It took several moments before the door opened. Celia's inky-black pate slopped out the doorway. Distance made dialogue indistinguishable, but then Celia screeched, "No-o!"

Beverly leapt to her feet, her eyes riveted on the woman collapsing in the doorway. *I better get over there!* Beverly sank back. *No... I better not... Not after that god-awful fight Mom and Aunt Celia had yesterday.* Beverly could still see their angry forms hovering over the picket fence, their angry faces nose to nose. She wrapped a strand of hair around her ear. *So many angry words... Can't believe Aunt Celia actually called Mom a graceless tank-topped slouch. Mom doesn't even wear tank tops. She was so-o-o mad! There's just too much bad-mouthing lately. It's just not like Mom at all and it's all because of that dumb ol' Jersey! Wish he'd just take a hike! We'd all be so much happier with him out of the picture.*

Quincy appeared in the doorway as the two plainclothes detectives lifted Celia to her feet. He held the door open as they hauled her into the cottage. He didn't go in right away. He just stood there. Then he sent a look in Beverly's direction—and it chilled her through and through—all the way down to her toes. *He knows I'm here!* She took a quick step back. Twirling to the left, she put her back to the wall beside the window. *He's thinking something awful! I just know he is!*

All those years growing up so close, Beverly sensed a weird connection between herself and Quincy. He sensed it, too—he told her so on several occasions. But lately, the squabbling between Pearle and Celia, all over Jersey Zayres, had put unpleasant distance between Beverly and Quincy.

But why do I feel like I should know what he's thinking right now? I feel kind of ashamed because I don't. No, not ashamed, maybe guilty? I suppose so. Guilty because I have absolutely no idea what he's thinking.

Moments passed as her senses reassembled. "Of course I'm here, Quincy," she murmured. "You and I have always been here for each other. How many times have we signaled each other with penlights in the night from our bedroom windows?" She shoved a wayward strand out of her face. "Now listen here, Quincy! I am no mind reader! And I haven't done one single thing to be ashamed of or guilty of, or anything!" A shiver raced through her. She took a deep breath and shook out her hands. "So what am I hiding for?"

Get a grip, Bev, raced through her mind.

"Quincy?" She peeked out the window. Her fingertips pressed against her lips. "He's not there!"

JUNE 7 - 11 A. M.

THE BEALE RESIDENCE

The scene at the morgue weighed heavily on Quincy as he elbowed open the kitchen door, his hands clutching a black vinyl trashcan. So absorbed in thought, he stepped out into a downpour. Lately, sudden thunderstorms had become daily rituals. *Can't believe Ma said that about Aunt Pearle. And now she's actually calling funeral homes! Comparing rates! She's actually going to pay for that jerk's funeral! Where in heck is she going to dig up that kind of money? She's already over her head with my college tuition. I should've gotten a student loan right at the beginning, but no, Ma wouldn't let me. And now—more than ever—I have to do everything she says! Don't talk to Beverly... What a rip-off! What did Ma see in that lying creep anyway? Feel like puking every time I think about him. I know it's wrong, but I'm glad the jerk's dead. He barged right in! Took over everything! Ma...our home... our whole life, for Pete's sake! Plus that, he snored like a pig! It's his fault Ma and Aunt Pearle fought so much lately. That last fight cut me and Beverly off completely. Everything is turned upside down. Nothing is like it's supposed to be.*

A lump stuck in his throat as he stewed over the previous night, the late hour when Beverly signaled with the penlight, persistent as the beam of a lighthouse in the darkness. There he was, lying in bed, trying to ignore the flashes on his bedroom wall, but in the deepest part of him... *I should've answered, but Ma's forbidden me from communicating with Beverly—and with Aunt Pearle. It's just not right. It's always been the four of us through thick and thin. I even thought someday I'd ask Beverly to marry me. I feel so complete when she's around. When I finish college and get a good job, I'm going to ask her to marry me. I will! Because I'll pay Ma back and then she can't stop me. Nobody will ever stop me from doing anything I want to do! But in the meantime... I just have to find a way to talk to Beverly. What a numbskull I was for not answering her last night. But Beverly, you know Ma watches me like a hawk. I'd be dead meat if she ever found out. For crying out loud, it's almost like Ma's gone and turned into Jersey herself!*

Lightning lit up the gun-metal sky as Quincy, oblivious to everything external, put the trashcan on the ground near the front corner of the cottage. *Ever since I can remember, I took out Beverly and Aunt Pearle's trash. Can't even do that anymore.* He lifted the cover off one of the galvanized garbage barrels. *Hate seeing them do it themselves.* He picked up the trashcan and was about to tip the contents into the barrel when he stopped cold. *What the heck is that? Is that Ma's favorite dress? It is! The purple one she wears on special occasions! Why is she trashing that?* As he pictured her wearing the purple dress on her first date with Jersey, his stomach turned. *That jerk went gaga over those cream-colored gloves she wore with it. Seemed a bit hokey to me.*

Quincy glanced toward the kitchen door, half-expecting to see the ever-vigilant eyes of Celia Beale. No sign of her. He set the trashcan on the ground and squinted at the dress. He scanned the rubble. A cardboard paper towel tube. He checked the kitchen door. His hand shook as he picked up the tube and unfurled the dress. He gasped. "There's her gloves! And the cream-colored shoes! Oh man, Ma's going to regret trashing all this." He glanced at the kitchen door. "Wonder if I should squirrel it away someplace so that..." His eyes knifed the outfit. "No! Absolutely not! No reminders of that creep!" He hurled the tube at the rubble as if it were a football then snagged the trashcan. In the midst of lifting the trashcan, he stopped cold once again. *That dress... It just might help Ma get over Jersey once and for all. And then maybe things will go back the way they used to be.* Again, he set down the trashcan.

"Don't know why I even care," he groused as he fished out the purple dress. He spread it over the dripping cover of a nearby barrel then picked out the gloves and shoes and placed them in the center of the dress. He rolled it all into a sodden purple mass then stuffed it behind the line of garbage barrels. "I'll come back for that later—after Ma goes to work. I just know she's going to want that stuff someday."

After dumping the trash into the barrel, he jammed the lid on and for the first time, became aware of the storm. Pulling his neck into his bent shoulders, he started for the kitchen door, but the sound of speeding cars stopped him. He straightened and glanced over his shoulder. "Cops!" He spun around. "Now, what do they want?"

The unmarked police car and two cruisers zipped past the Beale driveway. Relief sheeted over him. "Get a grip, man," he told himself. He set the trashcan on the ground. Wiping his hands on his navy blue soaking wet sweat pants, he stepped to the corner of the cottage and took a peek. The downpour was so bad that rain drizzled off his eyelashes. He could hardly see as lightning flashed and thunder rumbled.

"They're turning into Beverly's driveway? What are they..."

Quincy zeroed in on the plainclothes detectives getting out of the unmarked car. "That's Clement and Pomoroy! The same cops who showed up here yesterday and then at the morgue!" Suddenly, it all made sense.

"They're going to arrest Aunt Pearle for icing Jersey! I completely blocked out that part of it. Of course. I knew all along they were going to, but for it to actually happen..."

A blinding lightning bolt electrified the air. An instant later, earsplitting thunder. Quincy cringed. "Wait... What about Beverly?" His heart seemed to stop in the middle of a beat. "What's going to happen to Beverly? She's going to be all alone. She'll have nobody—not even me!" He spun around and put his back to the wall of the cottage. "Ma's definitely not going to let me help her—not after Aunt Pearle killed Jersey." His hands grasped his head. "But it's not Beverly's fault! And it sure isn't mine! This totally sucks!" He raised a fist to the storm. "How did all this happen? The four of us used to be so close! Beverly and I...so, so close! She's my guardian angel come down from heaven—an angel who knows my thoughts even before I do."

Nausea sheeted over him. "They're going to arrest Aunt Pearle..." He grabbed hold of the corner of the cottage and squirreled another peek. "Good God, Beverly, what in the world are we going to do?"

JUNE 7 – 11:15 A. M.

THE KEY RESIDENCE

Beverly pulled on her robe after showering in the downstairs bathroom, the only bathroom in the cottage. Towel drying her hair, she scurried upstairs to her bedroom. She was looking forward to watching the latest Leonardo DiCaprio movie she had ordered from Yellow Umbrella Books on Main Street in Chatham. Pearle was not a fan of DiCaprio or the roles he played. She claimed they made her squeamish. Still, Beverly owned just about all of DiCaprio's movies—and Elizabeth Taylor's, too. The actress' line of body products, White Diamonds, was the only one Beverly ever used. Pearle also claimed Beverly was obsessed with DiCaprio and Taylor. That's why Beverly usually watched the movies whenever Pearle pulled a double shift at the Rehab Center or covered for somebody who didn't show up for work.

Beverly glanced at the alarm clock on the white bureau. "Gee, Mom hasn't called. She must be pretty busy."

Just then, the doorbell chimed.

She stopped drying her hair and stepped to the window that overlooked the driveway. Nudging aside the pink ruffled curtain, she looked down upon four people who were standing outside the kitchen door. She tried to focus on the driveway, but the rain was so bad that she could hardly make out the form of a black car. The raucous storm was the reason she hadn't heard the car's tires crunching the crushed-shell driveway.

Lightning lit up the sky and the black car—and right behind it, a black and white cruiser. "Police?" She let go of the curtain. "This can't be good…" Her hand covered her mouth. "Mom!"

The doorbell chimed a second time.

She gawked at the henna-smudged pink towel in her hand, not quite seeing it. *Police are waiting for me to open the door. But Mom is always hounding me about not opening the door to strangers—especially when she's not home. But those guys down there look like real cops. And what if Mom got in an accident? Maybe she's in the hospital!*

At a loss of what to do, Beverly scanned her bedroom, the peaked ceiling, the walls—the upper half papered with pink roses; the lower half white tongue and groove woodwork—the honey-stained plank floor, the rocking chair from her baby days, the white canopy bed and bureau. All was a part of a childhood that Pearle was intent on preserving—well, except for the posters of Leonardo DiCaprio and Elizabeth Taylor plastered to the walls. According to Pearle, the bedroom belonged to Beverly since birth, so one of these days Beverly was determined to win the argument over redecorating.

Again the doorbell. This time accompanied by fist pounding.

She straightened. "Get a grip, Bev," she told herself. She tossed the towel across the foot of her white brass bed covered with the pink patchwork quilt Pearle had made. "Mom's okay, so go open that door before the cops bust it down."

She pulled on a pair of jeans and an aqua T-shirt then fluffed her hair with her fingers. Hand pressing her jeans and T-shirt, she exited the bedroom—as much as her heart told her not to. She paused on the top landing and peered into Pearle's lavender bedroom, a close distance whenever Beverly had a bad night. The bed was made. "The

36

bed is always made it seems to me. Mom is some busy lady, but she's never too busy to make her bed. She tells me that all the time just so I'll feel guilty and make my bed." Beverly heaved a sigh and clumped down the stairs. "Sure wish Mom was home. I just know she's not going to like me opening that door."

At the front door, she stopped and ran her hands up and down her thighs. She took hold of the door handle, slowly turned it, then inched open the door. She peeked out at a brown striped tie. *Coffee stains.* Behind the tie was a yellow shirt. *Coffee stains.* She zeroed in on the brown sport coat and trousers—sopping wet and all coffee stained. She squinted up at the face of a sallow-skinned, fifty-ish-looking man. Apparently, he didn't get outdoors much, though he was well built. *Probably works out at the station when there's no crime going on. That's the way it goes in Leonardo's movies.*

"Afternoon, Miss." The man tipped his hat. "I'm Detective Rodney Clement, Chatham P.D." He flipped open a black leather wallet and displayed identification.

She hesitated then opened the door—just enough to examine the badge and compare the snapshot to the round-faced Clement. She read the words, *Chatham Police Department.* Unsure what to do, she peered around him at three other men, one in street clothes and the other two in uniforms. All were hunched over—fighting not to be—in the deluge. *Are these the same cops I saw over at Quincy's house this morning?*

"May I bother you, ma'am," said Clement, "to allow my companions and me to step in out of this atrocious weather?"

She squinted at Clement who was blinking away the rain that slithered down his face. She felt bad for him, his companions as well. She gave a tentative nod then stepped back and swung open the door. She palmed the way into the living room.

As he entered, he removed his hat, showering her with rain. The balding detective gave her a mortified look. "Uhm..so sorry, Miss."

Tousling the dampness out of her freshly shampooed hair, she looked down and spotted the rain puddling around the feet of the four cops. She gave Clement a sidelong glance. He sent her another mortified look. She shrugged it off. "Don't worry about it."

Clement pushed back a tuft of hair that was stuck to the side of his face. "Are you Pearle Key?"

Beverly put her weight on one leg. "Mom's Pearle Key."

"Is she here?"

Panic rippled through her, all the way to her toes. "No-o..."

His head twitched side-to-side. Red splotches colored his pasty face and neck. Clearly, he was holding back some kind of disturbing information.

Rubbing her arms, she recalled Pearle's ivory oval face, which was now on the same level as Beverly's. Soft brown eyes, smiling, laugh lines—a sign of perfection in Beverly's opinion—she looked forward to having laugh lines. She could almost feel Pearle's generous lips at this very moment, pecking the usual sloppy kiss on Beverly's cheek. Then Pearle hurried out the door, late as usual. "Mom left hours ago."

"Actually, yesterday," said Clement.

Beverly nodded. "I've been so busy...school work..."

A younger male voice spoke up, "Do you know where we can locate Pearle Key?"

"I got a handle on this, Pomoroy," snarled Clement out of the corner of his mouth. Red splotches multiplied.

Breathing in spurts, she glanced at the young man standing off to the right of the detective. *Leonardo DiCaprio?* She wrapped a wayward brunette strand around her right ear. The stubborn Pomoroy, who appeared to be around her age, was cool as a cucumber. *Holds his ground pretty good against the old guy.* She met his eyes—the color of the maple syrup she slathered over Pearle's luscious buttermilk pancakes on Sunday mornings—so was his hair—a lot like her hair before Pearle doused it with henna. "M-mom's at...work...at the Rehab Center." She pried her eyes off Pomoroy and eyed Clement. "W-why? W-what's going on?"

The detective's expression divulged a noticeable distaste about responding.

Gooseflesh spiked all over her. "Mom is missing, isn't she?"

Clement flexed his shoulders. "Pearle Key did not report to work as scheduled. Neither she or her car can be located."

Beverly backed away, exhaling, "No..." Her brain rejected the entire concept. As she shook her head, cold, damp strands of hair slapped her cheeks. The world began to spin around her. She swayed like a drunk as her fingers dug at her temples to stop the throbbing and...

When her head finally cleared, Beverly found herself propped up on the living room sofa. Pomoroy was patting her cheek. She breathed in his spicy aftershave and liked it. *Not like that heavy stuff Jersey Zayres dumps on himself.*

Pomoroy withdrew his hand and glanced at his watch, the big kind that sport enthusiasts wore for more than just the time of day. He looked back at her, appearing to be in a hurry, but then a smile warmed his face.

She didn't know Robert Pomoroy from Adam and yet his presence made her feel less fearful. She peered down at his hand stroking hers and got the feeling that the worst was far from being over.

JUNE 8 – 8:00 A.M.

MEDICAL EXAMINER'S OFFICE

"The presence of Hank Night's fingerprints on the push broom is not by any means extraordinary," Curt commented. Bent over his desk, he was perusing lab results from samples taken at the murder scene. "As you may recall, Robert, I was present when he used it to manipulate the trash in the dumpster."

"First witness at the scene is always a suspect, Doc," Clement said, upon entering the cramped medical examiner's office.

Curt gave the detective a sidelong nod. "Rodney."

"Gives the witness an alibi, too," Pomoroy said. Then he added, "Rodney."

Clement eyed the young Fed who was sprawled like a jellyfish on the cushiest chair in the room. He eyed the large Styrofoam cup decorated with the burgundy and light gray logo of Chatham Coffee Company in the young Fed's hand. He grunted then took a gulp of coffee from a travel mug that had been through the dishwasher so many times that the red, white, and blue logo of the New England Patriots was barely discernible. Not as hot as he liked it. Not as fresh either. And not from the Chatham Coffee Company, voted best locally roasted coffee and deli on the lower Cape. He plunked himself down in the straight chair next to the door. "Have it your way, Pomoroy. But I've learned over the years not to ignore intuition when it's strangling my gut. I'm not about to ignore it."

"I was also a first witness at the scene," Curt said, obsessed with accuracy; a habit he had perfected during four and a half decades of life and many grueling years at the CDC. "Therefore, I am also a suspect, wouldn't you say, gentlemen?"

Clement and Pomoroy squinted at each other as their jaws dropped. Suddenly, they burst out laughing.

Curt cleared his throat—loudly. "I must say, the presence of Jersey Zayres' fingerprints is certainly quite curious, wouldn't you agree?"

The detective and the federal agent were suddenly quite humorless.

"Appears you both are of the same thinking—a rarity indeed," Curt said.

Clement grunted then took a sip of stale coffee. His teeth clenched at the taste.

Pomoroy casually put his feet up on the corner of the desk, crossing them at the ankles. He tipped the chair back onto its two rear legs.

Curt chuckled. "You two think alike whether either of you wish to admit it. However, each of you arrives at the finish point in dissimilar fashion. Be that as it may, impressions on the skull of the victim plus blood and hair trace on the push broom prove beyond any doubt that the push broom was indeed the weapon that incapacitated Mr. Zayres."

"Long enough for the perp to shove him into the dumpster," Clement added while setting his travel mug down on the floor beside his chair. "I have my doubts as to whether or not we have an intentional murder here." He looked up at the ceiling, never really seeing it, and scratched his chin. "By sheer coincidence, Zayres could have fallen on that metal corner protector."

"An unfortunate coincidence indeed," Curt said.

"Uhm...I don't think so," Pomoroy muttered.

Clement leered at the federal agent whose head was dropped back on the chair, eyes closed. He huffed then continued, "Several potential scenarios strike me. First and foremost, Zayres has the push broom in his hand." Clement acted out his theory as he spoke. "Now, if Zayres is merely toying with the broom, biding his time..."

"Biding his time on the loading dock," Pomoroy sniped. His eyes rolled beneath closed lids. "What is Zayres doing there in the first place?"

"Waiting for Pearle Key?" Clement offered as splotches of red peppered his face.

"Okay," Pomoroy breezed. "What's Pearle Key doing there?"

"To have it out with Zayres," Clement snapped.

Pomoroy snickered. "I'll get back to you on that one, Rodney."

The exasperated detective plowed on, "Pearle Key may have snapped."

"The operative words here are *may have*," Pomoroy said.

"According to Celia Beale," Clement said, "Pearle Key was lizard green jealous over the relationship between Beale and Zayres."

Pomoroy jabbed, "According to Celia Beale."

Clement postured, "Just wait until Pearle Key uses her credit card." He snapped his fingers. "I'll nab that woman just like that!"

Pomoroy opened his eyes and dropped his feet onto the floor. The chair came down on its front legs with a thud. "You think Pearle Key is actually that stupid?"

"She does have limited funds," Clement said, picking up his coffee mug. "Didn't take a dime out of her bank account before she left." He took a gulp that was obviously the last. "Didn't take her passport either."

Pomoroy stood up and stretched like an athlete before the Cape Cod Marathon. "What if the perp isn't Pearle Key? What if her absence is not related to this case at all? What if she ran off Route 6 in a deserted spot and wrecked her car? What if..."

"For Pete's sake, Pomoroy!" Clement dropped the empty mug on the floor. "No other car or resident has been reported missing anywhere on the Cape!" He drummed his thick fingers on his thighs. "And don't tell me Pearle Key went out for a walk and fell on rocks or in the water or anything else! Where is her car if she did? Plus! There are all kinds of folks out there! Combing every last square inch of Cape Cod! Posters of her face are going up all over the place! And so far, not even the slightest trace of her! Nada! Nothing! Zilch! It's like the woman never lived here in the first place!"

Pomoroy hooked his hands on his hips and faced Clement whose face was redder than the sunset during an August heat wave. "And why do you think that is, Rodney?"

"Who knows! Now stop analyzing everything I say, Pomoroy, and pay attention!" Clement took a deep breath, composing himself as best he could. "So then, a thief comes along... Zayres, having no reason to think he's about to get ripped off, puts down the push broom and turns his back. The thief picks up the push broom. Whack! He bonks Zayres on the head. Mind you, the thief was only intending to stun Zayres just long enough to steal his valuables, which now remain missing, and..."

Pomoroy cut in, "I don't buy it." He turned to the window.

Clement stared at the young Fed's backside. "You're some piece of work, Pomoroy." The detective's ruddy jowls jiggled like gelatin. He dragged a white handkerchief out of his pocket. "Feel like I'm nothing more than saltwater taffy being pulled and looped and folded over into itself." He swabbed his face, and jammed the handkerchief into his pocket. "Okay. Let's put Pearle Key and the other scenario on the backburner for now. There is another scenario that has Zayres knowing he's about to be attacked and thereby a struggle ensues. Zayres gets knocked off balance, kind of swings around, like this, and then he lets go of the push broom. The killer—and I say killer now because there's intent—grabs the broom and blam! A blow to the back of the head sends Zayres into the dumpster."

"In either case," Curt said, "the perpetrator must have been quite astonished when Jersey Zayres ended up impaled and mortally wounded in the dumpster."

Pleased to have the temporary medical examiner slash coroner on his side, Clement nodded. "In which case the perp takes advantage of the situation by climbing down into the dumpster and retrieving Zayres' diamond ring and earring, wallet, and who knows what else."

"Accordingly, the motive in those two scenarios is robbery," Curt said. "The next likely scenario, Rodney?"

"My thoughts are, Doc, that an addict—or addicts—were in desperate need of scoring. Perhaps Zayres placed too high a price on the drugs—so high that the addict couldn't raise the funds. Addict gets desperate—or pissed off—so when Zayres turns his back, the addict snags the push broom, bops Zayres on the back of the head then climbs down into the dumpster and takes all the drugs Zayres has with him. And while the addict—now a killer—is at it, he—or she—takes all the rest of Zayres' valuables. All we have to do is wait for some of those valuables to show up in pawn shops."

Curt drew back the side of his face, waving his head side-to-side. "Much needs to be done about the drug problem on the Cape. As it is, I discovered marijuana plants in the garden shortly after moving into my residence. The distinct odor of its smoke permeated the place until entirely being repainted and window treatments were replaced."

Clement sighed. "Keeping a garden of any kind is worth a medicine cabinet full of pills. Don't have time for any of that stuff anymore because of..."

"Another scenario," Pomoroy interjected, "is that there was an attempt to make the murder seem like an argument or robbery. Jersey Zayres billed himself as a kingpin of drug trafficking on the Cape and..."

"I was getting to that one," Clement snapped. He took the handkerchief out of his pocket again. "In actuality, Zayres was a second-rate hood who had designs on being a high-mucky-muck and the higher-ups were not about to go along with it."

"A mob hit," Curt mused as his thumb and index finger massaged his chin. "Ah, yes. I can see that as a distinct possibility."

"But there again, Zayres might've been blackmailing the killer," Pomoroy reasoned.

"And why's that?" Clement huffed, losing patience.

Pomoroy hesitated.

Clement wagged the handkerchief at the young man. "Come on, Pomoroy, out with it! You might be a Fed, cocky as a Rhode Island Red, but in this case, I say we locals take precedent!"

Pomoroy heaved a sigh. "For the most part, methadone is the drug of choice on the Cape."

"Stop skirting the issue, Pomoroy." Clement swabbed his face with the handkerchief. "We all know methadone is the leading cause of drug deaths around here."

"My personal opinion, Rodney, is that fentanyl is taking over," Pomoroy said. "In most cases, it's being illegally manufactured and mixed in powder form with heroin or combined with heroin and cocaine and then injected. O.D. stiffs ooze the stuff."

"Methadone is in greater supply," Clement argued, jamming the handkerchief into his pocket. "Reason is doctors overprescribe it all the time, which makes it readily available on the streets."

"I must say, my good man, I do take considerable umbrage to that statement," Curt said.

Clement squirmed; his chair creaked. "Aw, Doc, you know I'd never point a finger at you."

Curt hooked his chin. "Indubitably."

Pomoroy snorted. "According to police logs..." He turned his back to the window and stared at Clement. "...there has been a spike in fentanyl-related O.D.'s."

"Fentanyl is not new, Pomoroy. It's been around since the sixties."

"True," the young Fed said. "Hospitals use fentanyl in legal forms, in injections. It's dispensed as a slow-release gel through a skin patch or lollipop, usually for cancer patients. Drug users are getting their hands on the patches illegally and wearing them or ripping them open and ingesting the gel."

Though impressed by Pomoroy's knowledge, Curt was not surprised. He had known the young man since the tragedy at Granite Mountain, New Hampshire. Pomoroy was an undercover Fed—a Spiderling, the name terrorist Jonathan Aranea gave to his brainwashed victims. Pomoroy's performance was impeccable and highly admirable. It was just too bad that action had not been taken on his information and advice, thus averting casualties.

"Fentanyl is a potent narcotic," Pomoroy said. "It can even be dangerous for lab technicians, because while handling fentanyl, it might come in contact with their skin."

"Yeah, yeah," Clement slurped as his eyes rolled. "Enough with the lecture."

Curt and Pomoroy sent Clement sidelong glances and then peered at one another. Pomoroy continued: "Like I was saying, Rodney...fentanyl is being obtained either by theft or abuse by patients needing the drug for pain and become addicted to it. That's where the FBI comes in. I've been investigating the disappearance of fentanyl at the Rehab Center and..."

Clement perked up. "Hey, that's where Pearle Key works!"

"No kidding, Dick Tracy," Pomoroy said wryly.

Clement recoiled.

"Have you forgotten, Rodney, that Celia Beale also works there?" Pomoroy asked.

"Cut the crap, Pomoroy," Clement said. Then he winced. "It won't be pretty if that salty old dogfish gets hooked on our spool."

"It's not a matter of if," Pomoroy said, coming back to the chair he was seated in earlier. "It's a matter of when."

"Pretty scary, if you ask me," Clement said. "I got the feeling that woman can strip any one of us down to our spines quicker than an unlucky bluefish caught in a swarm of dogfish."

"Gentlemen," Curt said. "Let me remind you, Celia Beale was at work at the time of the murder."

After a time of reflection, Clement spoke up, "That was some crying jag the ol' biddy had...hands fondling the cheeks of that corpse like that."

"A certain sense about that entire scene was not quite right," Curt recalled.

"You can say that again, Doc," Clement said. "The way her hand meandered down his arm, beneath the sheet, then pulling out his hand; the way her eyes narrowed on his third finger." Clement attempted to mimic her:

"'Where's his ring? Jersey always wore that ring. And his diamond earring. What about his wallet? Is that missing, too? Where's all his things? His clothes?'"

Curt chuckled. "I dare say, Rodney, your imitation of Celia Beale is quite shoddy. Be that as it may, I detected a curious ring to her voice. Perhaps, it would behoove you to check out her background."

Pomoroy put his feet up on the corner of the desk. "Something doesn't add up in all this and I'm the guy who's doing the math."

"Cocky as a Rhode Island Red," Clement muttered, waving off the young Fed. "So what do you suggest, Pomoroy? Finding ourselves a drug addict and following him around until he leads us to the money and/or the drugs?"

Pomoroy dropped his head onto the back of the chair and closed his eyes.

"Gentlemen," Curt said. "Changing the subject, wouldn't you say Celia Beale's heavy use of henna is also a curiosity?"

"Eyebrows included," Pomoroy said.

"English women—typically those in Ms. Beale's age bracket—possess nary a qualm about allowing the natural decline of hair pigmentation."

"And what about the boy?" Clement said. "Blond."

Pomoroy scoffed. "Courtesy of peroxide."

"Young Quincy has a flair for the latest beachwear fashion," Curt said.

Clement shook his head no. "Mama dresses the little tadpole, Doc."

"Obvious wrinkles revealed the young chap dressed in a hurry before starting out for the morgue," Curt said.

"Who can blame the kid for sneaking out on the old biddy and sleeping the night away in less virtuous surroundings than that cottage," Clement said.

"Can't blame him for that," Pomoroy said. "But I don't think he has the stones to actually do it. And I don't think he has the stones to even begin to consider murder."

"He was ostensibly ill at ease," Curt offered.

"Not Celia Beale," Pomoroy said.

Clement winced. "She got downright mean there for a minute, didn't she?"

Pomoroy snickered. "Not only at Quincy."

"The woman certainly has a flair for the dramatic," Curt said. "I surmised at the outset that she is indeed an individual who recognizes a golden opportunity when she sees one. I say she was using Jersey Zayres to her benefit. Where young Quincy fits within that benefit appears to be quite hazy to me at the moment."

Clement sucked in a chest full of air and exhaled, "Like I said at the outset: First witness on the scene is always a suspect. So, the way I see it, Hank Night should have stuck around and helped to preserve the crime scene. After all, he is a janitor there. But no, the bum cuts and runs. Now, how does that look?"

JUNE 9 – 1:00 A.M.

THE KEY RESIDENCE

Beverly didn't sleep well—even after crying herself out. "Mom can't be missing? No. She can't be."

Strobic lightning blinded her as wind-driven rain whooshed against the windows as if emanating from an infuriated Neptune. His huge hands pounded on the shingled roof and then took hold of the cottage, rattling it for all he was worth. Over and over again, he thundered, *Pearle Key murdered Jersey Zayres!*

No way! her tormented heart cried out. *Mom would never do such a thing!*

Beverly shivered as within the chaos, Quincy's penlight flashes skittered across the wall. "I can't take it anymore!" she wailed, pulling the pink patchwork quilt over her head. "Go away! All of you! Leave me alone!"

But none of it went away. And Neptune was relentless, continually howling, *A cop car is across the street! Just wait until Pearle Key shows up!*

This can't be real! protested her heart. *No! It can't be!*

Real? Neptune roared. *There's no reality here!*

She grappled for her extra pillow then dragged it under the quilt and hugged it. "Come home, Mom," she moaned. "Please come home..."

6:00 A.M. - Beverly didn't get up the way she usually did. She didn't jog up to the beach and then with a mile under her belt, circle around and return home. She didn't shower, wash her hair, or plan out all the things she had to do that day. No, it was noontime when she finally hauled out of bed, bleary-eyed to a miserable gray day.

Somehow, she ended up dressed in blue denim shorts, white half-socks, and the sleeveless white blouse that she had bought last year in a boutique in downtown Chatham. "You liked this blouse so much, Mom." Gazing into the mirror on her white bureau, she fingered the eyelet cotton fabric. "I just had to go back and buy you one just like it. Remember? It's one of your favorites—because it doesn't show through your pink scrubs. Pink: the color of hope for cancer victims. Is there hope, Mom? When are you going to come home to me?"

Beverly picked up her white running shoes, her movement brittle and graceless, and wobbled across the hall. No sunlight filtered in through the window of Pearle's bedroom—only gloom. The bed remained untouched. The police didn't tear up the place the way it was depicted in movies.

"Everything is so still, Mom. So quiet. It's like you went on vacation or something—only you didn't take me."

She tried to draw in air, but there didn't seem to be any. She felt disconnected. Looking back over her life, it seemed every little thing had always been about the search for meaning and connection. Why? Pearle was the best mother anybody could ask for. Still, the feeling overpowered her. She looked over her shoulder, back toward her bedroom where the penlight beam had faded in the gray dawn. "Wish Quincy would stand up to Aunt Celia—be here to talk away this horrible stillness."

She dropped her shoes on the floor. Clunk. Clunk. Not even a crinkle of an echo.

She stepped to the closet, slid open the door, and stared at the clothes. Her hand reached out, touching, sorting. "Here's your pink scrubs, Mom." She unbuttoned the long-sleeved smock then took it off the hanger, leaving

52

the pants on the hanger. She held the smock to her face. "It smells like you. Soft—like you."

Memories throbbed throughout the countryside of her being: Pearle taking her to school for the first time; helping her with her homework; teaching her how to crochet; goofing off with her in the kitchen, cooking, washing dishes, mopping the floor. "So many smiles."

Beverly slid her arms into the pink smock then snapped up the front. She smoothed the fabric over her chest the way Pearle had taught her.

"Making a living is not the same thing as making a life," she whispered. "That's what you always told me, Mom. But I don't understand. How could you, my loving mother, leave me? Impulsive, hare-brained me? You left me to fend for myself? Who's going to pay the bills? Put food in the refrigerator? Gas up the car? Who's going to put henna in my hair?"

She turned and left Pearle's bedroom. Her brittle footsteps down the stairs sounded like that of an elephant's in the dreadful stillness. In the small kitchen, she slumped onto a chair, gazing across the round knotty pine table at the chair that Pearle always sat on. It looked so stark. "Nothing's changed, Mom. This table, the four chairs." She scanned the kitchen. "The cabinets and paneled walls still match. The linoleum on the floor still imitates white marble. Remember how you wished it were real? Well, the only thing that's changed, Mom, is you. You're not here, running around, trying to do everything all at once. Where are you? You're supposed to be here with me."

Beverly peered over her shoulder. Suncatchers still hung on the sliding glass doors that framed the backyard and Pearle's cherished sea and sky. Over the years, Beverly and Pearle had painted the array of shapes—birds, insects, sailboats, and so forth. Today, no sun brightened the shapes into rainbows that streaked throughout the room. Today, beyond the glass, the blue sea beyond the sliding glass doors was smothered in the foggy drizzle that replaced the chaos of the previous night. "You're out there, aren't you, Mom? Somewhere...beyond the glass..."

As a tremor shook her body, Beverly pushed herself to get to her feet. She shuffled into the postage-stamp-size living room. A small fireplace accented by white tiles portraying various nautical symbols in blue. Pictures above and beside the fireplace. Pictures of Beverly. Childhood pictures of her all the way up to the year she graduated from Chatham High School. Memories closed in around Beverly. She ran her hands up and down her arms. "This house is a cage to me, Mom. It's impossible to be here now and not have you here. I'm scared, Mom. I'm a trapped animal inside a cage—and I don't know what to do."

Beverly retreated backward. At the archway, unable to tolerate the emptiness any longer, she spun around and fled through the kitchen to the sliding glass doors. She grabbed Pearle's windbreaker off the hook, slid open the door, and barreled out onto the back deck. She stopped to stuff her arms into the windbreaker and zip it all the way up to her chin. Then she slid the door closed. "Okay, Mom, I'm not in the house anymore, so now what?"

She lifted her face into the overcast. It clung to her skin and eyelashes like Pearle's butterfly kisses. Lowering her gaze, she glanced around the deck where leftover moisture dripped like tears off the railings. Heaving another sigh, she pulled up the hood of the windbreaker and then crossed the deck, skirting chairs overturned during Neptune's wrath. She sagged onto the top step and wrapped her arms around herself. She rocked back and forth. Time passed without her noticing. "Where are you, Mom? How can you be lost on Cape Cod? It's so small—only a seventy mile stretch of land surrounded by ocean. And you've lived here for such a long time; you know every inch of the Cape blindfolded. Are you hurt? Out there somewhere? Crying out? Nobody hearing you?"

"Hi."

Beverly blinked.

"Are you okay?"

She blinked again. *Did somebody speak?* she wondered. *Or was it my imagination?* She glanced over her right shoulder. Her mouth dropped open. *Leonardo DiCaprio?*

"Didn't mean to spook you, Bev."

Slowly she stood up, staring at the young man with the maple syrup eyes and hair who had comforted her yesterday. His skin was the color of Indian summer—she didn't notice that yesterday. Hers got the same way by August. She pulled her eyes away from him, backing up the step, clenching her hands. "You think I know something about Mom."

Mild surprise lifted his eyebrows.

"Any minute now, your finger is going to poke me right in the face and you'll tell me you're taking me in for questioning."

He stared at her—the way he did yesterday.

"You're like the rest of them, aggravated, because I won't tell you anything," she said. "But I don't know anything!"

Get a grip, Beverly, flashed through her mind.

"Quincy?" Her eyes tripped along the white picket fence that separated the Key property from the Beale property. No sign of activity at the cottage next door.

"Bev?"

She inhaled, forbidding her eyes from meeting his, and tried to look composed, not about to fall apart.

"Don't know if you remember me or not," he said.

She nodded a faint nod. "You came here yesterday."

55

"Yeah. I never got the chance to formally introduce myself." He extended his right hand toward her. "I'm Robert Pomoroy, special agent for the FBI."

"FBI," she echoed, peering at his hand. It was a strong hand. Long fingers. Strong, capable fingers. *I don't want to shake his hand,* she thought. *My hand is so cold. My hand hasn't stopped shaking since Mom came up missing. He'll know right away that I'm a wreck.* She looked up at him. *But it looks like I have no choice.*

He frowned and started to withdraw his hand.

She snagged his hand. "Neither did I. I'm Beverly Key."

His frown smoothed away into a velvet smile. "Mind if I sit down, Bev?"

I don't know why I don't want to let go of his hand, she thought. *Maybe because it's so warm, just like it was yesterday. Maybe because I don't want to let his eyes look away from mine. Maybe because if I do, I'll break into pieces. Yes. I will break into pieces, I'm sure of it.* She shivered out the words, "I-I don't know where...where Mom is."

He looked away. "I'm not here about that."

She withdrew her hand.

He sat down on the top step and looked up at her. "I just wanted to see how you're doing."

"Why?"

"I was worried about you, that's all."

"Why would you be worried about me? Uh-huh, this has to be a ruse. You're here to get information about Mom. She's gone without a trace and you think if you soft-soap me, I'll spill my guts."

He was quiet for a while.

"Silent company is often more healing than words of advice—that's what Mom always says," Beverly said. "Slick, Mister Federal Agent. Real slick."

He ran his hands up and down his pant legs, ignoring her remark. "The sun's punching through the clouds," he said.

"Your voice is so calm, soft and easy, low—probably makes you one of the best investigators in the whole wide world," she said. "Bet you can modulate the tone of your voice just so, make it gentle, soothing, or mean and vicious—whatever's necessary to get the job done."

Again, he ignored her remark. "Won't be long before things warm up," he said.

"Smiling down on us," she added, surprising herself. "Uhm... Mom says that about the sun all the time."

His hand patted the step beside him.

She studied his hand and then looked into his eyes.

He smiled at her, warm, sincere.

She rubbed her hands up and down her thighs. "It's as if the storm last night never happened—as if Mom isn't missing." Hope rushed like the high tide into her heart. "Any news?"

His expression turned downcast and his soulful eyes looked away from her. His head waved side to side. "I checked just before I got here. The trail is totally cold."

She stepped down and wilted beside him. "Mom didn't kill Jersey."

"There's not an ounce of doubt in your voice," he said.

"Why should there be? Mom can't even kill a bug. If she finds a spider crawling up the wall, she gets a newspaper and uses one of the pages to force the spider to climb onto another page and then she goes outside and lets the silly thing go in the long grass."

He made a clicking sound. "Doesn't make sense, Bev."

"No, it doesn't." She drew in a chest full of air. "Look, I can see you're not a bad guy. You're just trying to be a hero and I'm being a jerk. Speaking of jerks..." Her vision moved to the gate between the driveways. "How could Aunt Celia say such a terrible thing?" Her mind's eye saw Pearle and Celia arguing. "The four of us used to be so close. One big happy family until..."

Pomoroy cut in, "Pearle and Celia are sisters?"

Beverly shook her head. "Just act that way. Aunt Celia is the bossy one. She and Mom sometimes went head to head about that. Guess it's the way it is with sisters. Never had one though..."

Pomoroy was thoughtful for a moment. "You and Quincy..."

She read wariness—or perhaps a little bit of jealousy—into his question. She sensed an inner suffering. It hung over him like it wasn't entirely new to him. Had there been someone else? Once upon a time? She cleared her throat and said, "Quincy and I..." Without warning, one of those transcendent moments struck her. She had them at the oddest times. Moments of quick realizations. Connections that were impossible to explain. "We grew up together."

"Like brother and sister," Pomoroy added.

She stared at the cottage next door. "Until recently."

A long moment passed. "Until recently?"

She nodded.

"What does Quincy have to say about it?"

She shrugged. "Nothing." She wrapped her arms around herself again and began to rock back and forth. "When Aunt Celia and Mom started fighting over Jersey, Aunt Celia didn't let Quincy come near us anymore. Now that she says Mom murdered..." Beverly put her face in her hands and sobbed.

Pomoroy wrapped an arm around her shoulders and gave a light squeeze. "We'll get things figured out, Bev."

She swiped moisture away from her eyes, peering sideways at him. "You don't think Mom murdered Jersey, do you, Bobby?"

He gaped at her.

She tilted her head then blinked at him. "What?"

"Nobody ever called me Bobby before."

"Oh..."

His gaze softened. "Uhm...I...I guess it's okay."

"Did anyone ever tell you that you look like Leonardo DiCaprio?"

He chuckled. "No-o-o," he said in a singsong voice.

She chuckled, too. It was a small, rusty chuckle, but it was a real chuckle, and it felt strange—and good—but given the circumstances, it also felt wrong. Guilt swept over her.

"Bev?"

She hung her head. "Tell me the truth, Bobby."

"I'll always tell you the truth, Bev."

"Did Mom really murder Jersey?"

She looked up at him. He was scanning the sun-drenched sky. She followed his line of sight. In the distance, three multicolored hang gliders were circling, rising and falling within a thermal, creating an odd sort of rainbow.

"My gut says no, Pearle Key did not ice Jersey Zayres." He winced. "My gut also says there's more to this entire situation than meets the eye."

Summer And August

JULY 13 - 11:00 A.M.

THE BEALE RESIDENCE

"Whoever got that jerk's stuff will fence it sooner or later and that's when the cops will finally make some progress," Quincy said. He was slouched over the keys of the antique upright player piano placed kitty-corner in the small living room. His fingers plinked out sour chords.

"But it's been more than a month, honey," Celia whined while putting the lid on a plastic container. She was about to leave for work.

"Don't remind me," Quincy grumbled. "Pomoroy's been dropping anchor at Beverly's every day since Aunt Pearle took off."

"What was that, honey?"

A wave of his head sloughed her off as the smell of lemon pepper chicken and broccoli over pasta with pesto sauce made him gag. *Ma makes that pukey mush all the time. I'm sick of it. And I'm sick of the smell of that perfume that jerk gave her. Why is she still dumping it all over herself?*

The sound of a car entering the driveway caused his fingers to freeze on the keys. His glance out the window turned into a glare. *Pomoroy! Again!* As jealousy stabbed Quincy, his stomach somersaulted. *Just look at that 2005 Viper. Copper. SRT-10 8.3 L V10. 6-speed. And a convertible to boot! Beverly's got to love that! No way can my clunker of a pickup compete with that.* He tugged his eyes away from the window and mumbled, "Get a grip."

"Your lunch is in the fridge," Celia said. "And don't forget to take out the trash. I don't appreciate doing your chores. I have enough on my plate."

He barely heard her as his insides continued to fume. *I should be the one with Beverly. I should be the one comforting her. Loving her. Protecting her. Not that Pomoroy. I've been part of her life from the very start. Beverly and me. Aunt Pearle and Ma. It's only natural that the four of us should always be together. Always. When Aunt Pearle gets back, it's going to be that way again. Aunt Pearl won't take things being like this. And she won't like that Pomoroy hanging around Beverly either. I know she wants me and Beverly to be together. And I'm sure as sure she didn't kill Jersey. She doesn't have a killing bone in her body. Wish I could prove she didn't do it. Don't know how though... Wish I knew how to make things go back the way they were. Don't know how to do that either—especially with Pomoroy trawling the neighborhood. For crying out loud, Aunt Pearle, get your butt back here right now!* He swallowed hard. *Please?*

Beverly's sweet voice filtered in the window. "Come in, Bobby."

Quincy rolled his eyes. *Bobby—what a sissy name to call a Fed.* He gritted his teeth, battling the urge to look out the window again, knowing that if he did, the image of Beverly and Bobby together would reduce his living and breathing memories to ashes. *'So many good times just memories.' Ma used to tell me that over and over again after Jersey arrived on the scene. 'And you know, honey, it's all because of Aunt Pearle. She can't stand Jersey. Well, screw her!' Well, maybe that's still true for Ma—her memories may be dusty with passing time—but that's not how it is with me. My memories are clearer than clear, happening right now, moment by moment. The four of us—Ma, Aunt Pearle, Beverly, and me—enjoying the sunshine of an early spring day, picnicking on Monomoy Island in the sweltering heat of August, catching migrating butterflies in the fall, playing Scrabble in front of the fireplace during nor'easters.*

"Sure could use the cash that diamond ring and earring could bring," Celia whined.

Quincy banged his hands on the piano keys, horrified to discover he was gazing at Beverly's kitchen door—the door Pomoroy just passed through.

"What is wrong with you, honey? You have been moping around since the moment you got out of bed."

"Nothin', Ma."

Her footsteps grew loud behind him then stopped. He heard her teeth grinding the way they always did when something pissed her off. Her fingers ran through his hair, pulling up clumps, reviving that bed-head image she loved so much. "You need to get back to your studies, honey."

He pulled away from her and got to his feet. Perching on the windowsill, he linked his arms across his chest, glaring at her.

Celia sucked in a chest full of air then turned back to what she had been doing. "All that cash tied up at the funeral home and that blasted coroner just won't release the body for burial."

Quincy had everything he could do not to scream, *Get a grip! If you didn't shell out all that cash just to plant the jerk, you'd have some cash!* He took in a deep breath and squeezed out, "Listen to me, Ma. It's highly doubtful that Jersey's stuff will ever be turned over to you. It isn't like you were married to him, you know. And any day now, some long lost relative is going to come out of the woodwork and claim it all."

"It belongs to me!" she snapped. "I earned it! Every last penny!"

Somehow, Quincy wasn't at all surprised to see Celia get her back up.

Suddenly, her angry face turned into a frown. "I mean...you and I earned it... honey. We put up with a lot of crap from that Jersey...now didn't we?"

Quincy gawked at her.

She blinked hard at him and then once again backpedaled. "Oh, gosh, honey, what a terrible thing for me to say." Her eyes fled to the heavens, as did her gesturing palm. "Sorry, Jersey."

Just then, a giggle arose on the breeze. Without thinking, Quincy turned and glanced out the window. Beverly was on the back deck, looking up at Pomoroy, smiling sweetly. A sledgehammer of disappointment came down hard on Quincy. *How many times has she smiled at me that way? Those sapphire eyes of hers looking at me that way? Twinkling in the sunlight? I just know she's lost in that Fed.* He sagged onto the piano stool. *And she's lost to me...* He felt as if half his heart had just been ripped from his chest, leaving the other half behind, feebly beating out a pulse.

"What in the world are you looking at?" Celia demanded. She marched over to the window. There was a pause then he felt her eyes bore into him. "For pity sake! Have a little pride and stop ogling that fickle brat!"

He turned and placed his fingers on the piano keys. It was impossible to hide the pain of losing Beverly.

Celia grabbed him by the shoulders and spun him around. "Look at me!" She latched onto his chin and made him look into her eyes. "I said, 'Look at me!'"

He met her eyes.

"You are much too good for that idiot girl!"

He didn't respond.

Her chin jutted out. She let go of him, throwing up her hands and looking away. She stiffened her back and seemed to grow taller. Her eyes locked on him. "Listen, honey, you've got better things to…" A noise prompted her to look out the window. "Now what's going on over there?"

Quincy followed her line of sight. Special Agent Pomoroy was taking a tray of picnic supplies from Beverly. Both of them were wearing Chatham A's baseball caps, sunglasses, white shorts, and blue strappy T-shirts. Quincy felt his brows fuse. "He's wearing a gun."

Celia waved it off. "Feds pack guns all the time."

Beverly turned and headed back into the cottage. Moments later, she reappeared, a tray of beverages in her hands.

Tires grating on the driveway drew Quincy attention. Out of the corner of his eye, he noticed Celia's eyes narrowing. "Now who can that be?" she asked in a voice that could have crushed those driveway shells worse than any tire ever did. Her lips pursed as she watched a metallic green 2008 GMC Envoy slow to a stop behind the copper Viper and red VW. When the driver got out, Celia gasped. "It's that coroner! What's he doing over there?"

Quincy watched Doctor Curt Shirlington dart around the Envoy and open the passenger-side door. The woman who got out was quite pregnant. "Must be his wife."

"Must be," Celia growled.

As the smell of a heating grill drifted into the window, she spun around and crossed her arms, tucking her hands under her armpits. "Can you beat that? That little tramp is giving a barbecue! Pearle's gone a month and that tramp is having a whoop-de-doo party with that Fed *and* the coroner! *And* his wife! Of all things! Beverly should be ashamed of herself! Like mother like daughter, I say…"

Quincy banged on the piano keys. "Stop it, Ma!"

But Celia raved on, "I just don't know what came over Pearle. Jersey was so kind and…"

Quincy jumped off the piano stool. "I said stop!" His eyes impaled hers.

She stepped back, ramming into the windowsill. She sat down on it hard.

"Aunt Pearle did not kill Jersey!" he cried. "You know she could never do a thing like that!"

"But honey, you have to believe me," she whined, her brow furrowing slightly. "Pearle did it."

His fists clenched. "Get a grip, Ma! Someday the truth is going to come out! Just wait and see!"

Her palms came up at him, waving. "Okay, honey. Okay. Let's just not talk about it anymore. Okay?" She stood up from the windowsill. "Why don't we…"

Mirth filtered in the window. Quincy wanted to puke. He sagged on the piano stool.

"U-uhm…" Celia stuttered. "W-why don't we… Tell you what, honey, you… You need a haircut. How about when I get home, I… I will cut your hair…and I'll do your roots. Time to bleach out those roots again. Yeah, that's what we'll do when I get home. My goodness, honey, your hair grows so fast! On the way home, I'll stop by the drugstore and pick up…"

"No, Ma." He gasped out the words. "No more bleaching."

"But, honey, please. You have to."

"I don't have to!" He rotated toward the piano, pressing his fingers on the keys. "And I'm getting a haircut! Tomorrow! At Wes' Barbershop on Queen Ann Road! I've heard he does the best flattop in Chatham!"

"Flattop?"

He glared over his shoulder at her. "You heard me!"

Horror filled her eyes as the back of her fist jammed against her mouth.

He looked back at the keyboard, lowering his voice. "I am always trying to please you, Ma, but this is one battle I am determined to win." He glanced out the window. "Look at Beverly. If she isn't coloring her hair anymore, why should I?"

Celia didn't come to the window, although calm returned to her voice. "You know she won't let anybody but Pearle do her hair."

Quincy looked back at Celia.

She began to pace. She wagged her index finger in the direction of the cottage next door. "It's high time that brat did something about her hair. That orange is just horrid!"

He stood firm, his fingers plinking piano keys. "If Beverly is not going to color her hair anymore, neither am I. Nope. From now on, I am going to be me—the way I was meant to be."

Summer And August

JULY 13 - NOON

THE KEY RESIDENCE

"Nice to meet you, Doctor and Mrs. Shirlington," Beverly said, adjusting the visor of her Chatham A's baseball cap.

"Please, call me Penny," the very pregnant woman said. She hooked her thumb over her shoulder. "And he's the old fuddy-duddy."

Curt fired a look at his wife, his brows jumping to the headband of his Red Sox baseball cap. His light blue, short-sleeve shirt, open at the collar, was tucked precisely into his navy blue cargo shorts. White socks rose out of black Rockport shoes and ended below his knees.

Penny winked at him and then at Beverly. "You better call him Curt."

He smiled at his wife. "That flowery muumuu and floppy, wide-brimmed straw hat you have donned this day lends you the appearance of having recently arrived from an island vacation."

"I wish," Penny quipped, peering down at her hand circling, caressing her distended belly. "Truthfully, this pregnancy has been a kind of vacation. Nine months almost done, and no complications at all—not even morning sickness. Modern medicine has certainly made motherhood a dream come true for women like me over the age of forty."

Robert Pomoroy elbowed Curt. "Fuddy-duddy?"

"Aye, my Penny is the dear one, is she not?" Curt breezed, as the pungent smoke of a hot grill tickled his nostrils.

Pomoroy turned toward the railing of the deck and out of the corner of his mouth, said, "Penny is exactly what Bev needs, Curt. Anything to lighten the pall that she's been under since Pearle's absence."

"History has shown my Penny is very good at that sort of thing," Curt said, leaning on the railing next to the young Fed. He put his weight on his elbows and looked out over the backyard. Beyond, above the limitless Atlantic Ocean, a colorful hang glider was drifting within a thermal.

"Took a lot of persuasion to make this day happen, Curt. It was only a week ago that I was finally able to talk her into a short jog on the beach with me. She used to run a couple miles just about every day."

"Resuming everyday activities will certainly do the lass a world of good," Curt said.

"Always the optimist," Pomoroy said.

Curt hooked his chin. "Be that as it may, Robert, this case is unsettling. In all these weeks, not the minutest hint of where Pearle Key might be."

"Not so much as a rumor," Pomoroy said.

Curt made a clicking sound. "Indeed unsettling." He waved his head side-to-side. "Does not bode well for Pearle Key, I fear."

The two men stood silent, staring at the hang glider.

"You must envy that individual strapped into that glider, Robert."

"A little maybe. I sure did a lot of weird stuff while tracking down terrorists—hang gliding included. Some of that stuff is supposed to be peaceful entertainment, but for me, it came with the territory—do or die."

Beverly's voice attracted their attention. "How about a glass of iced tea?"

The two men straightened, turning away from the railing as Penny quipped, "A gallon if you have it." Her hand was still circling the mound of her stomach. "And I strongly advise you to show me the most direct route to the little girl's room."

"Right now?" Beverly squawked. She looked to be on the verge on a full-blown panic attack.

"Nah," Penny said, waving her free hand. "It's only been five minutes since my last trip. I think I can wait five minutes more, but don't take bets on it."

Curt chuckled. "It would behoove my dear wife to get off her feet." He gestured to a white metal chair that matched three others at the round table beneath a blue striped umbrella.

"Good idea," Penny said, waddling to the chair.

Curt dashed for the chair and held it as Penny lowered herself onto it.

She smiled up at him and then at Beverly and Pomoroy. "I'm warning all you guys right here and now that after ten minutes, it'll be a dead run for that bathroom, so don't any of you get in my way."

Pomoroy used his right pointer finger to nudge up the rim of his Chatham A's baseball cap. He winked at Beverly. She smiled a thin smile, which instantly vanished at the sound of a door slamming. Horror sheeted her face as she, along with Pomoroy, Penny, and Curt, zeroed in on the cottage next door where Celia Beale was stomping to her black Saab.

"Don't you dare forget to take out the trash, Quincy," Celia hollered. Skirting the back of the Saab, she added, "Or you'll be dead meat when I get home!" She yanked open the door, hurled herself into the driver's seat, and slammed the door.

The engine turned over, revving to fever pitch. Tires kicked up shells and white dust as the black Saab bolted backward all the way to the street. Upon hitting blacktop, the tires screeched, then screeched to a stop, then screeched a third time when Celia jammed the gearshift into drive. Off went the Saab, fishtailing down the street and out of sight.

The racket died away. Birds began to tweet.

Curt took off his cap and waved away white dust. "I say, that was an adventure."

Penny made a face that resembled a prune. "Something's got our adorable Celia Beale all riled up."

Beverly shivered. "Get a grip," she muttered, wrapping her arms around herself. "You know, Mom has a black Saab. Just like Aunt Celia's. But nobody can find it. Mom neither."

Curt sent a rueful glance at Pomoroy.

The young Fed returned the glance. Bracing his backside against the railing, he cleared his throat. "So, Penny," he said, "when did you say you are due?"

Penny adoringly eyed her stomach. "Any minute now."

Beverly stiffened. "Really?"

Penny giggled and her belly jiggled. "I'm joking, Bev! I'm joking! But soon—I hope."

Beverly's entire frame wilted with relief. "Do you know what you're having?"

Penny patted her belly. "An elephant."

Beverly blinked hard. The corners of her mouth slowly lifted and then she burst out laughing. Her levity, rare since Pearle's disappearance, was so extraordinary that Curt, Penny, and Pomoroy couldn't help but join in. As tears diluted the tension of the past weeks, Beverly caved onto the chair next to Penny and tore open the package of dinner napkins. She snagged a wad of the napkins and mopped her face with them. Penny, Pomoroy, and Curt did the same. When at last they pulled themselves together, Beverly sputtered, "Bobby says this is your first baby."

Penny, in the midst of blowing her nose, nodded. "Kind of glad it's a boy, even though the ol' fuddy-duddy and I wouldn't have been heartbroken if it was a girl."

"A male will keep the Shirlington name going," Curt boasted.

"But a girl will keep the family tree growing," Penny puffed.

"There is that, my dear wife."

"So what's the kid's handle?" Pomoroy asked.

"Jeffrey Curtis Shirlington," Curt crowed.

"Jeffrey was Curt's father's name," Penny interjected. "You know, Bev, Curt and I are both at the end of our family trees. I've been doing some research though, and have had some luck on both sides—lots of second and third cousins whom we intend to look up after J.C. is born. Curt's father didn't have siblings on record. I'm still tracing him. Another week or so and I'm hoping to start tracing his mother."

"That's a lot of work," Beverly commented. Sadness returned to her face as she glanced down at her hands folded on her lap. "Looks like I'm the last of the Key family tree. My mother says there's nobody left but her. I asked her about my father—he ran off before I was born. She says she never did marry him. She says she heard he died in a car crash in California. I don't even know his name."

Penny took hold of Beverly's hand. "Your mother will turn up."

"It's so hard when there isn't so much as a trace of her," Beverly said.

"Everything possible is being done to locate her," Curt said, observing the washed-out color of Beverly's ponytail.

"There are posters with your mother's picture everywhere," Penny added.

"I know," Beverly murmured. "There's lots of support, but still..."

Watching Penny comfort Beverly, Curt recalled a similar scene when Summer and August LaRosa were abducted. *There was just no comforting Adam and Janice. Similar to this case, much effort went into locating those wee ones with nary a trace of success whatsoever. So many dead ends in this life.* He heaved a sigh and got to his feet. "Walk with me, Robert?"

"Where to?"

"I am off to retrieve that genealogy tome from the Envoy for my dear Penny."

When out of hearing range of the two women, Pomoroy said, "Things are going pretty good, huh?"

"Indubitably, ol' chap. I am immensely pleased to see you and the lass are content with one another."

"Didn't think I'd feel this comfortable in a relationship," Pomoroy said. "If that's what you call it. Under the circumstances? Know what I mean?"

"Keep a steady heading and think positive thoughts," Curt said, leading the way between Beverly's faded red VW Bug and Pomoroy's copper Viper. "I am sure the past will..."

Pomoroy cut in, "Look, Curt, Katrina and I are history. She and I were always trying to be superheroes—in our own way—selfish and pigheaded."

"I would not label either one of you as selfish," Curt said. "Pigheaded has merit."

"One way or the other," Pomoroy said, "it just about impossible for Katrina and me to come together."

"So, now all that's over," Curt said.

"Sure looks like she and Casey are into it for the long haul," Pomoroy said. "So I'm moving on, too."

"I sense no bitterness," Curt said, taking his keys out of his pants pocket.

"None at all." Pomoroy lifted his cap by the brim and wiped the sweat off his brow with his forearm. "No sense rehashing the past."

"Life has given you a second chance," Curt said.

"Yup," Pomoroy said. "Say, Curt, I got a question for you."

"Out with it, old man."

"Do you think I look like Leonardo DiCaprio?"

Taken aback, Curt sputtered, "I say!"

"Bev keeps saying I look like him."

Curt analyzed the young Fed. "You are more angular." He chuckled. "However, I dare not be so bold as to enter into a debate with the fairer sex."

Pomoroy ran his hand through his hair. "I'm no movie star who's played cushy roles, that's for sure. Wish I were. I'm so fried—burnt out—not just with all the terrorism I've handled, but also with all the moronic crap humanity deals out to itself. I just want to climb out of the muck and get on with life. I want to live, not just participate in life."

"Are you considering resigning from the F.B.I., Robert?"

Pomoroy settled his cap on his head. "I thought investigating drug peddlers on the Cape was going to be a breeze. As usual, I was wrong. I still think about Granite Mountain and all those kids—Spiderlings—like it happened only yesterday. Alice... What a waste. You know, sometimes I catch myself humming the song, *Go Ask Alice.*"

Curt felt his gut knotting. "Eidetic memory will do that to a bloke." He opened the passenger-side door of the Envoy. "A day does not pass without me thinking about the circumstances surrounding Granite Mountain. As I see it, grief is like the tide, rising and falling, a torrent at times, gentle and warming to the heart at other times."

"Yeah, but it's time to shift priorities," Pomoroy said, hooking his hands on his hips. "I just can't blow this thing with Bev."

"Are you sure, Robert? Or are you just running from memories and Beverly is your gateway to a quick escape?"

"I'm not much good at romance, Curt, but this time, it's real. I know it is."

"Odd how one can open one's eyes and there is one's soul mate—quite accidental—at a time when one or both needs a soul mate the most. Aye, it happened that way with me—and I am pleased to see it has happened to you, Robert."

Pomoroy leaned against the front panel of the Envoy. "But just like before, I have competition."

Curt leaned over the seat, grabbed the genealogy book, and backed out of the Envoy. "My dear, young man, your meaning eludes me."

"Don't look, Curt, but Quincy Beale is watching us. He's in the front side window."

Curt shut the door and while handing the book to Pomoroy, caught a glimpse of Quincy in the window of the cottage next door. "Indeed, young Mr. Beale does have a bead on us."

Pomoroy opened the book, pretending to be discussing it. "Creeps me out the way he plants himself in that window and watches everything that goes on over here. He's obsessed with Bev—I just know he is—and I've invaded his territory."

"Have you spoken with him, Robert?"

"Not sure how to approach him. He hasn't spoken a word to Bev since before Pearle disappeared. And you know what else, Curt? Celia Beale ran the show around here."

"Ran the show?"

"She paid the bills—not only her own, but also the bills incurred by the Key household. And if repairs or anything else came up, Celia Beale took care of it. I know because a week ago, Bev asked me to help her figure out a stack of bills. Bev says that's just the way things were, but you could have bowled me over with a feather. I just don't have any idea how to tell her that I'm investigating Jersey Zayres' drug-peddling operation at the Rehab Center." Pomoroy closed the genealogy book and handed it back to Curt. "How do I tell her Pearle Key and Celia Beale are tied into it? I'm going to need a ton of proof before upsetting Bev any more than she already is."

"So you have not been forthright with the lass about your suspicions."

"Not as much as I'd like to," Pomoroy said. "She's been so down about Pearle still being AWOL. I'll do anything not to add to her troubles."

Curt pretended to be perusing the back cover of the book. "Anything significant in Celia Beale's or Pearle Key's background?"

"Not one shred of paper exists about them before they moved to Chatham," Pomoroy said. "Nothing about where they came from. Every document, I've seen—birth certificates, educational documents—all are fake. I bet my life on it. And they bought these cottages within a month of each other."

"And each paid cash," Curt deduced.

"You got it," Pomoroy said.

"At the very least, Beverly must be made aware that the connection between Pearle Key, Celia Beale, and Jersey Zayres is not based solely upon jealousy," Curt said.

"But if the investigation keeps going in the direction it is, Curt... If I turn up proof at the Rehab Center that those two women supplied..."

Curt finished Pomoroy's thought, "Any future relationship you have with Beverly may very well be in jeopardy." He put a hand on the young Fed's shoulder. "I empathize with your dilemma, Robert."

"Bobby!"

Pomoroy gawked at Curt. "Bev?"

"Doctor Shirlington! Come quick!"

"Well, I say!" belched Curt, taking off to the back of the Key cottage like a shot.

"Hurry up! Penny's water broke!"

AUGUST 15 – 5:00 P.M.

KATE GOULD PARK

Trudging into Kate Gould Park from Chatham Bars Avenue, Hank Night felt weak and queasy. His eyes rarely focused, swinging back and forth like pendulum discs. His brain wasn't functioning much better. The stink of his sun-baked skin meant nothing to him since his sense of smell had cut out on him a long time ago. His filthy T-shirt, which, once upon a time, was white, clung to him. His knee-worn, faded black trousers were riding up his butt, not to mention the running shoes he had plucked out of the dumpster at the Chatham Inn and Conference Center were half a size too small.

Oblivious to passersby eyeballing him for talking to himself, he grumbled, "Can't tolerate summer. August: blisterin' heat one day; sky-high humidity the next. Then comes bone-chillin' blow off the ocean."

He swiped grimy sweat off his face with the back of his hand. "Sure am countin' on coolin' these blistered heels of mine in the cellar of that there Yellow Umbrella bookstore. Ain't been down there since Jersey got spiked. One stormy night that was. Can't understand why that stinkin' Jersey had to go and get so nasty. Ain't no dealer now anywheres on the Cape that'll take my treasures instead of cash like Jersey did."

Several yards into the park, three mid-life workmen were haggling next to a broken down lawn tractor. Hank couldn't make out their words, but he knew what the bright red can in one of the men's hand contained—Coke. Coke of another form would ease Hank's misery. "With luck, I got another hit of Jersey's poison in that there cellar. Countin' on it. Duck into that dark nook o' mine and take a little trip. Let that owner and his em-ploy-ees come searching' for some e-lus-ive book. Ain't none of 'em ever gonna catch wind o' ol' Hank in that there nook. Comes to be one o' my favorite hangouts every time I get canned. And man, did I get canned hard this time. Held that job at the Oceanside since before Jersey got spiked. Up 'til today. Long time for ol' Hank." His eyes fell to the ground, downcast. "Holy cow, did that prissy manager blow his top or what when out of nowheres, my gut explodes. All over the foyer I just mopped up. Ol' Hank's gonna hafta find a way o' cashin' in treasures pretty quick 'cause..."

A bash on the shoulder sent the homeless man spinning like a tilt-a-whirl at a county fair.

An unfamiliar voice blasted, "Hey, watch where you're going, idiot!"

By the time Hank recovered some sense of balance—and what little eyesight he had left—whoever had chewed him out was lost in the throng gathering around the gazebo to hear the Chatham Band.

Swaying this way and that, Hank found himself facing the building that housed the public restrooms. The day the doors first opened, someone scrawled on the building: Acrapolis. Hank knew the guy who did it. "Real smart-aleck. 'The building is said to be reminiscent of the Parthenon in Greece' is what the guy kept yammerin' on and on. I kept on tellin' him the only Greece I know is what's on bacon I pick out of trash barrels." Hank glared one last time at the building then swiveled away from it. "Can't even take a decent piss."

He staggered toward Main Street. "Ain't nobody gonna find those treasures I got stashed in that cranny behind that stone in the wall. Jes' waitin' on the right time and place to market it all. Bonus is rumors circulatin' amongst drifters such as myself that ghosts haunt that there cellar. Keeps treasure hunters at bay, that's a fact. Ghosts... What a pile of malarkey."

He stopped at the fountain and gulped down a mouthful of water. He spat out half of it, gagging, and then mopped his lips with the back of his hand. "There for a minute, I thought my guts were gonna follow." He sucked in air—that's when he noticed the kid with a skateboard chucked under his arm.

"You're disgusting," the kid sneered. His face reeked of sharp disdain.

Hank popped his eyes at the kid and grinned a yellow tartar grin.

The kid just stood there. "Am I supposed to be scared?"

Hank gave a feeble wave of the hand. "Prissy kid."

He trudged on. "Detest all of 'em. Kids. Tourists. Dog-day-summer people. Squat houses. 'Specially on days like this. Every square inch of ground's overrun with 'em. Dark alleys of Beantown is the place losers such as myself can make a living, no questions asked. Those treasures of mine's in high demand. No doubt about it. Shame I can't go now. Too soon. Time oughta get a move on. Aye-yup, move yer fat butt, time. I gotta ditch this here Cape and do some dealin'."

A coughing fit seized Hank. He stopped, hacking up phlegm that stretched from his mouth to the ground. His index finger plowed it off his bottom lip, but then it stuck to his hand. He flicked it, once, twice, and then it took off into the air, squirming like a night crawler that escaped the beak of a robin in flight.

He stumbled on. "Too pukey to go to Beantown. Where's that do-gooder Doc when a sicko needs him? Bah!

81

Ain't even strong enough to bum over to Hyannis and hop the dinner train to Sandwich. If I got that far, I'd get to Beantown for sure. Oh, well… Most I need right now is a good hit—somethin' better'n booze…shroud the sickness…take the sting out of living off the streets…off this broken back…"

Matters worsened when Hank closed in on Main Street and spotted the broad-shouldered bicycle cop across the street, hanging out in the alleyway next to Yellow Umbrella Books. "Last thing I need is gettin' caught in fuzz-boy's crosshairs."

The homeless man made a left onto the crowded sidewalk along Main Street. One of the many times he got arrested for vagrancy drifted across his brain:

> The cop shoved a statement in Hank's face.
> "Can't read," Hank told him.
> The cop bellowed, "Whaddaya mean, ya can't read?"

Hank grunted. "Whole bunch of 'em gawks at me like I'm some kind of freak."

Born Henry Nuit, he was seven years old when his family moved to the Boston area from their native Montreal. At his new school, the French-speaking, second-grader never quite mastered spoken English. The written word totally eluded him. Teachers were relentless though: cajoling him; scolding him; threatening him; smacking him. No matter how hard the he tried, he couldn't make heads or tails of the black lines and shapes. Year after year, despite failing grades, he got promoted. What did his parents say? "'Never gonna amount to nothing,' that's what they said," Hank grumbled. "'Won't stack up to a pisshole in a snow bank.' Humph. Always signed my report cards. Real disgusted-like."

So the once outgoing and friendly Henry Nuit retreated into a protective shell, keeping to himself most of the time, never fitting in, few friends—if any. "Lonesome life for a kid," Hank muttered. "Learnt ta make myself invisible. Long before ever graduatin', I did just that! Just disappeared! Been Hank Night ever since."

The clog of foot traffic swirling about him brought his belly to his mouth. He choked it back.

"So I'm e-lit-ter-ate. Screw it. Nobody's ever gonna know, not if ol' Hank can help it."

At the crosswalk, he turned toward the street. Pausing, he dug his fist into his knotted chest.

"Plus side is me havin' a first-rate memory. Directions I get down in a heartbeat—who lives where, what treasures they got. Make a tidy living off the streets—that I do. I can write my name—that's enough. Bluffed my way along mostly. Can tell a word here and there by sight: go, stop, enter, exit, whiskey—ah, whiskey..."

He swiped his hand across his mouth. "Droolin' worse than a Saint Bernard."

He checked out the bike cop. "Nope. Ain't gettin' busted for nothin'."

He stepped into the street. "Bluffing ain't always useful—never could get a driver's license."

Halfway across Main Street, Hank felt like a block of C4 exploded inside his head. He stopped in his tracks, digging his gnarly fingers into his skull.

A horn blared. Tires screeched. "Get out of the road, you nincompoop!"

"Up yours," Hank slobbered, without so much as a thought or a glance at the hood of the car that was less than an inch away from his left leg.

"Out of the way or I'll call the cops!"

"That ain't good," Hank mumbled as out of the corner of his right eye, he spied on the bicycle cop down the street. "Better get a move on." He ambled to the opposite side of the street.

Stepping onto the sidewalk, he wheezed, "Gotta score something strong that'll stifle all the crap inside this here head of mine."

In the alley between the block that housed Yellow Umbrella Books and the Chatham Squire Restaurant, he thought he caught the scent of fried cod. "Wish I had the funds to stop into the Squire and sink my chops into a heaping plate of that luscious fish." The titillating young ladies who usually seated Hank in the furthest darkest corner of the place didn't appreciate his appearance much. Neither did anybody else. Nevertheless, eating was the farthest thing from his mind this day as dizziness swamped him and his heart thumped so hard, the pain so bad, that he toppled against the building. Puke rose in his throat then erupted in a putrid stream that splattered the brick building that was baking in the sun.

"You all right?"

Hank sucked in air and squinted over his shoulder. Several feet away, a stringy dude in baggy madras shorts, maroon T-shirt, and funny straw hat, was holding his sunglasses above his eyebrows to get a better look at the ailing man. Behind the dude was a starchy female who had a couple of snot-nose brats in toe. Hank eyeballed the lot of them then spat on the pavement. Their eyes bugged out. The female hastily reined in the brats and herded them off. The dude let his sunglasses drop over his eyes and trotted after them.

Hank shoved himself away from the building and struggled to take in air while waiting for equilibrium to kick in. Neither had come close to remedying itself before he dizzily shambled off to the rear of the building.

"With luck, the door's propped open." He knew all the back doors that were propped open on days when the weather was good. "Bet dollars to donuts, today's too hot." He rounded the back corner. "Wouldn't cha know—air conditioner's a-buzzin' like a bee on sea roses. Hmm. But cha know what? Even on bad days, most backdoors ain't locked. If timin's right, I'll slip right in, nobody the wiser for it. If timin's bad... Well, that there owner'll run me off right quick. Maybe even call fuzz-boy while he's at it."

Wobbling through the parking lot, Hank took quick glances over his shoulder at the backdoor of Yellow Umbrella Books. Upon reaching the alley that ran beside the bookstore, he spotted the bicycle cop's backside. The cop put his mouth to the cell phone that was clamped to his shoulder then spoke a few words. He straightened and put his weight on the right pedal. No sooner did the cop take off than the bookstore owner came out the backdoor.

Hank veered off, almost losing his balance. A hand gripped him by the arm. Next thing he knew, he was looking into the steel-blue eyes of the bookstore owner.

"Are you all right?"

Aghast, Hank took a quick step back, yanking his arm free. He steadied himself on a parked car and swallowed hard. "Heat's got to me," he wheezed. "Car'll cool me off right quick." He wormed his hands into his pants pockets. "Got keys...right here...in one of these here pockets."

Panic zinged through Hank as he wiggled his fingers then pulled out the lining. Gritty lint took wind. He peered at the expressionless face of the bookstore owner. He looked him up and down. "What the devil you mullin' on?"

Without a word, the bookstore owner turned and walked off, disappearing down the alley that paralleled Main Street.

Hank scrambled to the backdoor of the bookshop. Looking this way then that, he peeled his ears. "Clear." He slipped into the backroom where cool musty air smacked his overheated face like the open hand of his fourth grade teacher. He struggled to pull in air, to keep his head.

A second door lay ahead of Hank. It was propped open with a stack of books. Beyond it were rows of books— for which Hank had no use at all. A customer, nose planted in a book, didn't notice the homeless man slithering to the left toward the cellar door. Arthritic fingers of both hands gripped the door handle, turned it, and clamped the wooden railing on the right just as he was about to plummet headfirst down the stairs. He did not feel the splinters that invaded the skin of his fingers and palms.

When Hank got to the bottom of the stairs, he sucked in air, reveling in the dank odor of crumbling boxes, century-old wood framework, and walls made of stone. He wobbled to the far end of the cellar. Behind a stack of boxes, he stopped and fished a switchblade out of his pocket. Crouching down, he pressed the button on the handle of the switchblade. The blade slid out. Along with his filthy, broken fingernails, he used the switchblade to pry a basketball-size stone out of place.

The stone crashed onto the floor. He froze, ears peeled. He grinned a yellow tartar grin. "Nobody heard nothin'." His voice was nothing more than slush now.

He squinted into the hole. "Sure beats burying treasures in backyards I might never get back to." Sliding the switchblade into his pocket, he neglected to retract the blade. He reached into the hole and extracted a treasure wrapped in a cleaning cloth he had found upstairs after the storeowner left for the night. "This is gonna fetch ol' Hank big bucks on the streets of Boston." He placed it on a stack of boxes and squinted into the hole again. "Can's still here."

As Hank struggled to dislodge the rusted red A & P Coffee can, the fingernail of his index finger tore off down and beyond the quick. He didn't notice the pain. He didn't notice the blood. When at last, he got the can out of the hole, he clamped the can between his bicep and forearm and grappled with the plastic lid. Fingernails pried, bleeding, as he dug at the lid until it peeled away. He squinted inside the can. He jostled the contents. "All here, 'cept Jersey's poison. Used it up, I s'pect." He heaved a sigh. "Gonna be a long night." He replaced the lid then stepped on top of the can to make sure the lid was secure. He picked up the can, slid it into the hole, and then put the treasure wrapped in a cleaning cloth back in.

Hank struggled to pick up the stone that seemed to weigh a lot more than it did only moments ago. Managing to get it wedged back into the wall, he then fell back on the stack of boxes, out of breath, head pounding. He contemplated the wall through foggy eyes, shivering and scratching his grungy chin. He gawked at his fingers, mistaking blood for sweat. "Shiverin' and sweatin'."

He turned to the stack of boxes and dropped to his knees. Gripping the sides of one particular box, he dragged it out just enough so that he could crawl into the small nook he had constructed the first time he slinked into Yellow Umbrella Books.

A small plastic bag was lying on the floor inside the nook. "Jersey's poison," he wheezed, picking up the bag. "Been wonderin' what happened to you." He held the bag to the light. "Not much left. S'pose it'll do." His grimy, bleeding, spindly fingers labored to open the bag then he tipped the contents into his mouth. His index fingers plowed every last particle onto his tongue.

He tossed the bag out of the opening then dragged the box in behind him. The entry to the nook was now plugged. "Nobody's ever gonna find ol' Hank cooped up in here."

Half-blinded by infirmity, darkness, and Jersey's poison, Hank trawled his pocket for the switchblade. Though the open blade slashed his fingers, he felt nothing.

In the midst of carving his initials and the date into the wooden beam in the center of the nook, he paused. "What's that?" A glint of light caught his eye again. "Well, I'll be." He folded the blade into the cowl—or so he thought he did—then he dropped it on the floor. The blade gouged his knees, time and again, as he groped around until finally locating a bottle. His gnarly fingers held it up its neck close to close to his eyes. "Looky here. Must've left this here last time. Merlot. No problem readin' letterin' on booze." He shook the bottle. "Half full. Thank the devil that made me."

His empty stomach erupted as he worked at the cap. At long last, he got it off. Choking back vomit, he took a huge pull and grimaced. "Tastes like Grandma's vinega'." His bloody hand scoured his lips. "Vinega's better'n nothin'."

Heaving an acidic wheeze, he noticed circles of lights. "What the..."

The lights swarmed closer to Hank.

"Ghosts!"

A whoosh of pain struck the homeless man like a meteor and then darkness, blacker than the devil's soul, came down hard upon Hank Night.

AUGUST 16 – 4:00 P.M.

YELLOW UMBRELLA BOOKS

According to Penny, the owner of Yellow Umbrella Books was a lot more knowledgeable than he let on—"That is, once Eric warms up to another person."

For some reason, my dear spouse absolutely adores the bloke, Curt thought while easing the Envoy into a parking spot in front of the bookstore. *The feeling appears to be mutual, since during their conversations, in which I am present, I sense I am nothing more than a fifth wheel.*

Main Street was quite narrow in the compact center of Chatham, so Curt double-checked the side mirror before opening the car door. Walking was the preferred way to get around for residents and tourists—the same mode Indians used in the 1650s when the first white settler, William Nickerson, came down from Plymouth Plantation and haggled with the Monomoyick Indians to obtain rights to scythe the marsh hay inside the outer beach. Incorporated in 1712, Chatham, like so many towns throughout New England, was named after a town in England.

Curt stepped around the rear of the Envoy and then up onto the front porch. Upon opening the door to the twenty-eight-year-old full service literary bookstore, he inhaled. *Ah, the sweet stuffiness of prose.*

He weaved between bookshelves of classic literature, art and nautical works, and regional books. *I have no doubt as to the accuracy of Penny's statement that this bookshop is one of the best-known destinations on the*

Cape. She claims Eric, a native Cape Codder, has seen his share of tourists and nor'easters of which he is of no mind to discuss. Yet, according to Penny, he has the most incredible Yankee humor and a quick mercurial smile. I find it disquieting that I fail to recognize any humor whatsoever in the man. Needless to say, when I told her that, she got huffy. "You're just not paying enough attention to see it, that's all!" I also find it disquieting whenever Penny gets huffy. Her chin juts out sharper than the elbow of the Cape into the great Atlantic.

"Good morning, Doctor Shirlington."

Curt shot a glance at Eric's slender wife who was standing behind the service counter framed by current fiction, poetry, bookmarks, and children's books. "And a good day to you, Patty," he said, tipping the brim of an invisible hat.

"Eric is in the office," she said, winding a tress of her sandy blond hair behind her right ear.

As a customer placed a book on the counter in front of Patty, Curt headed to the back of the store. He heard the cash register drawer slide out with a ding and then Patty's fingers rummaging in the drawer for change. Paying no mind to that or to the cookbooks, gardening books, and a growing collection of used, rare, and out-of print books, he continued to muse: *Apparently, Eric's humor often goes unheeded. I do however recall a particular incident when he articulated a witticism. Penny immediately burst into boisterous laughter—much to my chagrin. After much deliberation, I am still at a loss to find the slightest humor in that articulation. Curious, though, the look of shock that overcame the man upon seeing Penny's response—the silliest grin then lit his face and it was brighter than the Chatham Light on a crystal clear night.*

Eric was scouring paperwork at an antique oak desk. Workable clutter scattered the surface. Curt recognized the light purple pocket T-shirt, white duck pants, and brown sandals the trim man was wearing; all products of L. L. Bean.

"A good day to you, sir," Curt said.

"How are Penny and the baby doing?" Eric asked with a preoccupied toss of the head.

Curt was taken aback. *At the very least, I should receive a return greeting,* he thought. *The bloke certainly has a one-track mind.*

Eric looked up, his ice-blue eyes spilling over the gold-rimmed half glasses perched low on his nose.

Only Katrina's Siberian Husky, Mickey Blue Eyes, has eyes of such hue, Curt thought. *Quite intense blue. Wonder if his eyes also turn red in the dark.* The chair creaked and Curt found himself locked in Eric's gaze. "Er...fine," he blustered. "Penny is just fine. Jeffrey is also fine. Picture of health. Whale of an appetite."

An efficient smile—that quick mercurial smile of which Penny spoke—elevated the right corner of Eric's mouth—Curt nearly missed it. This time, he was paying attention. *Penny will be delighted.* He waited for Eric to speak—per her instructions. *"Eric is a person who gives a great deal of thought to what he is going to say before he opens his mouth," she claims. "More people should be that way."*

Resolved to hold his tongue, Curt continued to wait. Time moved at a snail's pace. *Nobody will ever accuse this chap of being effusive—then again, rightfully so. In days gone by, people took time before speaking. None of this jibber-jabby nonsense one hears these days. Ah, yes, life used to be so much slower, so much simpler. People got to know one another—the very reason Penny and I relocated to Chatham. Unfortunate indeed that I have become caught up in a murder case. Bah, I cannot tolerate this silence one moment longer!* Words surged from Curt's mouth like the tide that breached the outer beach during the "no name" storm of 1991. "Penny sent me for that genealogy book she asked you to order for her."

Eric picked up a brown paper bag perched on the right corner of his desk. "I have it right here."

"Why am I not surprised," Curt muttered, rolling his eyes. *Another man would be jealous,* he thought. *However, I know Penny well enough. If there were a burgeoning base to this mutual admiration society, she would not—or could not—hide it from me.*

Those steely eyes skipped over the gold-rimmed half glasses, piercing Curt.

At a loss as to what to say, Curt opened his mouth as if to speak, but as he did, a fetid odor ambushed him. His nose tracked the odor. It was coming from somewhere over his shoulder. "I say, that is indeed an unpleasant stench." Receiving no response, he looked back at the storeowner who seemed to be pondering the perfect word.

At length, Eric said, "Obnoxious."

Curt twisted up the side of his face and made a clicking sound. He turned and stepped into the backroom. "It would seem that Chatham's sewage disposal system may be in sad need of repair."

Sticking his head out the open backdoor, Curt sniffed to the left. He sniffed to the right. "Not a trace of odor." He pulled in his head then turned into the backroom. He caught the unwavering gaze of the storeowner who was still seated at his desk, leaning to one side, neck craning around the doorframe, half glasses perched on the tip of his nose. Curt tugged his eyes away.

He peered into the restroom where the toilet and sink, though dated, were well scrubbed. The trash bucket was empty. The floor was swept and mopped with a cleaner that left a shine on the vinyl tile that had seen its share of traffic. A small wicker basket, filled with vanilla potpourri had been placed on the toilet tank to lend a pleasant scent to the air.

His fingers splayed across his hipbones as Curt rotated into the backroom. "I say, the stench has to be emanating from within this building." He squinted to his left. "What lies beyond that door?" Receiving no reply, he glanced at Eric.

Still seated at his desk, still leaning to one side, rubbernecking, icy eyes streaking over those gold-rimmed half glasses, the storeowner was totally absorbed, mouth small and tight, in the doctor's explorations.

Curt cleared his throat, the strident way his English father employed to gain attention.

Those icy eyes came to life, focusing on the door. After a moment of contemplation, Eric rose from his desk and stepped over beside Curt. Those icy eyes never left that door. At length, Eric said, "The cellar."

"It behooves us to investigate, wouldn't you say?" Curt asked.

"Be my guest," Eric said as his palm gestured ever so slightly.

Well, now, that response was indeed on the hasty side, Curt thought.

Upon opening the door, the vial stench intensified. He jammed his nose and mouth into the inside of his left elbow. His stomach turned as he looked back at Eric.

"Light switch is on the right," Eric said, his voice stifled by his hand that was covering his mouth and nose.

Curt peered at the dark wooden stairway digested halfway down by a windowless cellar. He pushed up the light switch. A single bulb, dangling over the landing below, lit up the stairs and the wall on the left fashioned out of stone and cement. To the right was a rough-hewn wooden railing, which stirred images of splinters invading the palm of his hand. "I'll not be lying my hand on that railing anytime soon."

"You might want to avoid going down there," Eric said.

Leaning toward following that advice, Curt glanced at Eric. "Why is that?" Then, tongue in cheek, he added, "Is the cellar haunted?"

Eric's words were halting, "That is the rumor."

Curt hooked his chin. "I assume the spirit is that of an unrequited lover?"

"Something like that."

Curt tisked. "How would it look if rumored ghosts deterred further investigation?" He eyed the darkness below then took the first step down. "'Tis a cruel ghost indeed who casts off such disagreeable stench." Descending the stairs, he tried to ignore the high-pitched creaks; he tried to ignore the storeowner behind him, sticking close to him, albeit a bit too close.

"A guy who clears buildings of ghosts came down here a while back," Eric said, his voice cracking.

After a moment, Curt said, "And…?"

"He detected male ghosts that have been down here since the early 1900s."

"I trust they have an affinity for women," Curt said, again tongue in cheek.

"Correct," Eric said.

"Correct?"

"One ghost has it for tall women," Eric whispered. "He wields torture devices."

Curt echoed, "Torture devices."

"Another ghost refuses to move on after being spurned in a love affair," Eric said.

"The object of his affections was a person who once worked in the building," Curt assumed.

"I have one heck of a time getting employees to come down here," Eric said.

"I am not surprised," Curt said, "considering the stench that permeates the air."

"The stink is new!" Eric spat. "I would never put up with a thing like that!"

"Sorry ol' chap. I meant no offense." Curt strained to see. "If it is at all possible, the darkness appears more intense down here than it did at the top."

Without warning, a second light blinded Curt. He turned to see the silhouette of Eric, looking very much like a ghost, backing away from a switch attached to a stair post. "My dear man, you might have notified a fellow spelunker."

Inching along between two rows of old boxes and miscellaneous storage items, every so often, Curt lifted his nose from his elbow and tested the air. The putridity was intensifying—to the point that it was irritating his eyes.

At the far end, Eric whispered, "This corner is where the spurned lover hangs out."

Curt turned to the right. "Forewarn me, my good man, when you sense the presence of any apparition wielding torture devices." He pulled up quick, pointing at the stone wall. "A good-size scorch blackens this wall."

Bumping into Curt, Eric gasped, and hastily backed away. "Did you say scorch?"

"I imagine that more than a small moment of panic erupted when the apparition attempted to squelch the flames," Curt said, bending at the knees and scrutinizing plastic pouches, straws, and needles that littered the floor.

Eric edged past Curt. "Smoking is not allowed anywhere in this building."

Curt stood up. "Perhaps the ghosts are smoking."

"Give it a rest, Doc," Eric said as his hand dropped from his mouth and nose. "Good Lord! What a stink!" His hand clamped his mouth and nose.

Curt pushed aside a box half-filled with books. "Is that an empty vegetable can?"

"Nobody is allowed down here without my specific instruction," Eric said, using his left hand to pick up the can. He read the label. "Cream corn?" He peered inside. "Marijuana and tobacco butts."

Curt inspected the wall. "This particular stone has been tampered with." He crouched down. "Scratches. Chips." His eyes widened. "Blood."

"Looks like blood drops on the floor," Eric said.

Curt reached into his pocket and pulled out a pair of blue surgical gloves. He held his breath while wedging his hands into the gloves. He took off his button down sweater and held it against his nose. Breathing normally, he tied the sleeves behind his head.

"You made a mask," Eric said. He looked down at his T-shirt. "I can't do that with this!"

Curt gave a one-shouldered shrug, raising his eyebrows. He turned back to the wall and dug his fingers around the edges of the scarred stone.

Eric tapped Curt on the shoulder. "Here, use this."

Curt squinted at Eric's hand and then up at him. "Pocketknife?"

"What's the matter?"

"You carry a knife?"

"A Yankee tradition," Eric said.

Curt took the pocketknife. "I suppose if I carry around surgical gloves, you are entitled to carry a pocketknife." He drew out a blade then wedged the tip of it between the cement and stone. Knife and finger worked at the stone until it fell on the floor. He peered into the hole. "Cleaning cloth?" He reached in. His fingers gingerly probed the cloth. "I say, the cleaning cloth conceals…" He took it out of the hole, placed it on a stack of decrepit boxes, and peeled away the cleaning cloth.

Eric gasped. "A gun?"

Curt looked into the hole again. "A coffee can has also been sequestered in here." It took several moments to dislodge the can then Curt reached in for it. He pried off the cover with the blade and peered into the can. "Well, I'll be…" He straightened then stepped over to the stack of boxes where the gun was lying and tilted the can. A diamond ring skidded out. He jounced the can. Out came a diamond stud earring, a watch, an empty money clip, and coins.

"Where did all that come from?" Eric asked.

Curt met the storeowner's eyes that were watering from the stench, just like Curt's. However, in the dim light that shimmered off gold rims, the ice blue eyes glowed bright red—redder than those belonging to Mickey Blue Eyes ever did! "Well, I say…"

"Now what's the matter?"

Curt cleared his throat. "I presume the items belonged to Jersey Zayres."

"The dead drug pusher?"

"One and the same."

"How did those things get in that hole?"

Curt scanned the cellar. "I assume that the very same individual who murdered Jersey Zayres stashed them in that hole."

"Murderer? Down here? When? How…"

Curt cut off Eric, "Give me a hand with this stack of boxes." He removed the top box and placed it on the floor a short distance away.

"Look, Doctor Shirlington, moving things around is not what I have in mind. This cellar may look disorganized, but not to me."

Curt relocated another box.

"Oh, all right," Eric huffed. He held his breath as with both hands, he snagged a box. He placed it on top of the stack Curt was building then covered his mouth and nose with his hands and sucked in air.

In the middle of picking up another box, Curt stopped. His jaw dropped.

Eric pressed closer. His eyes, big and round, met Curt's. "It's that vagrant I ran into in the parking lot yesterday."

"Hank Night," Curt said, scrutinizing the homeless man lying in the fetal position wrapped around a wooden beam. Initials and dates had been carved into the beam. Dehydrated blood, vomit, and excrement fouled the nook.

"Don't tell me he drank that stuff," Eric said, gawking at the bloodied plastic bottle of drain cleaner in Hank Night's hand. Eric began to gag. Realizing he had once again dropped his hands from his mouth and nose, he quickly rectified the situation.

"Cuts on the thumb and index finger," Curt said, frowning at the gnarly fingers that held a death grip on the bottle of drain cleaner. He scanned the homeless man. "Left hip of his pants is lacerated—also the left knee of his pants—quite severely."

Eric pointed to a bloody switchblade. "The blade is extended."

Curt bent at the knees, avoiding the pool of dehydrated blood as best as he could. He probed the homeless man's neck for signs of a pulse. "Hank, ol' man."

A meager deepening of breath.

Eric gasped. "He's alive?"

"Hank," Curt said, prying open one of Hank's eyelids. "Can you hear me, ol' man?"

A scant groan.

"Call 911, Eric," Curt said, without looking up. "Do make haste, my good man, for this poor fellow is in dire need of medical attention—more than I can accommodate in such putrid environs."

Summer And August

AUGUST 16 – 7:00 P.M.

REHAB CENTER

"Wake up, Night!"

The husky male voice, full of echoes, rippled far away in Hank's mind.

"Come on! Open those eyes! Good God, Night, you stink!"

Hank's mind resisted the here and now as his tortured lungs struggled for air and pain saturated every fiber of his body. A steady bleeping in the background made his head ache worse than any hangover he ever had.

"You killed Jersey Zayres," charged the husky voice.

Hank pried open one eye. Within bleached-out haze, shadows undulated. Instinct compelled him to run, but his body refused.

"You stole his wallet, his diamond earring, his diamond ring..."

Deep inside Hank—as if from the devil's furnace itself—his guttural voice skulked like molten magma, "R-i-n-g..."

"Always coveted that ring, didn't you, Night?" jeered the husky voice. "It's one of many reasons why you killed that dope-dealing good-for-nothing."

"Sh... o..." wheezed Hank. Feeble coughs failed to rid his mouth of a filthy, acidic pollutant.

"Showoff—that's right, Night—Jersey Zayres was one big showoff! Always flaunting what a big man he was.

101

Fancy duds. Always flaunting that gaudy ring and earring. Always..."

"Go easy on the ol' boy, Rodney."

"Doc?" choked out the homeless man, struggling to focus.

"That is correct, Hank—Doctor Shirlington here."

The homeless man felt a warm, reassuring touch on his forearm.

"You are in the critical care unit at the Rehab Center," the doctor continued. "The beeping you hear are monitors tracking your vital signs. Every so often you will feel the blood pressure band on your upper right arm squeezing."

Squeezing? Hank tried to say; however, the word floated only through his mind as if driftwood on the tide, never quite surfacing.

"Detective Clement here wants you to clarify the circumstances that led to the demise of Jersey Zayres."

"Let me at him, Doc," said Clement. "I know how to handle this kind of good-for-nothing fish bait."

"A moment if you will, Rodney," said Curt. "As I see it, Hank has been on guard all his life. He has always devised up-to-the-minute excuses, evading the facts in order to protect himself—to cover up the truth. Am I correct, Hank?"

Truth... Bitter regret twisted the homeless man's face.

"Ah, my dear ol' boy, 'tis indeed a terrible way to live."

"There's a latent criminal in all of us, Doc," sniped Clement. "Decades of pounding the beat have taught me that. So now, out with it, Night! You killed Jersey Zayres and stole his belongings, didn't you? You couldn't live with it, so you decided to off yourself. But Jersey's fentanyl cocktail wasn't fast enough to do the job, so you decided to guzzle down drain cleaner."

Drain cleaner? churned through Hank as his strength melted away.

"I say, Rodney, badgering is rather callous of you. I place you above such action. A bit more finesse, if you will."

"You know very well, Doc, that finesse is just not up my alley."

"Indeed. Did you read Hank his rights?"

"Get a grip, Doc! I cover all the angles!"

As oblivion stalked Hank Night, he attempted to clear his throat. Next thing he knew, Clement was growling close to his ear, "Don't have guts enough to tell the truth, isn't that right, Night?"

Truth...

"Hank did not have the physical and mental prowess to overpower a man of Jersey's enormity," said Curt. "His physical prowess is the reason I lent him a hand cleaning up after the seminar."

"Now look, Doc..." Clement's stale coffee voice moved away from Hank. "To fish bait like this, evasion is synonymous with living. Isn't that right, Night? Well, I got news for you, old man. You are dying. You know you are. So admit it. Confess your mortal sins before you reach the other side. You don't want your soul spending eternity with the devil, do you?"

"I say, Rodney! That is quite enough!"

Hank drew a shuddering breath. "Aye-yup."

The doctor gasped.

Surprise that warped the detective's voice. "Aye-yup? Aye-yup, you killed Jersey Zayres?"

Hank struggled against a buzzing swelling inside his head.

"Say it, Night! You killed Jersey Zayres!"

As shadowy faces of everybody Hank had ever known surrounded him, his head shifted...up...and then down... Faces melded into eyes drawing closer and closer. Voices... Screeching...

"Come on, Night, 'fess up."

The shadowy eyes exploded into dust. Screeches sailed into a sea of silence.

His eyes closed—and for Hank Night, it was for the last earthly time.

AUGUST 17 – 9:00 A.M.

CHATHAM POLICE STATION

"That is correct, Ms. Lawless," said Curt, watching the reporter from the *Cape Cod Chronicle* scan the just-issued police report. Fair skin, green eyes, blond hair, and facial structure conveyed a Swedish ancestry. Her perfume was familiar—possibly the same that Beverly Key used. "I never suspected for an instant that Hank Night murdered Jersey Zayres. His confession boggles my mind."

"Not mine," spoke up Detective Clement.

"Is that because Hank Night was homeless?" asked Lawless as she took a reporter's pad and a blue Flair Pen out of her emerald green pantsuit. "A regular fixture in the Chatham area? Therefore overlooked as a suspect?"

"The homeless population on the Cape—as well as across the entire United States—is indeed a grave matter not to be overlooked," said Curt.

Clement huffed. "You two can't be serious. We just nailed a murderer who happened to be homeless and now you're going to dredge up excuses for him so that the public will bawl its eyes out for him? What about the victim here? I know Zayres wasn't anything to write home about, but come on."

"There was a time that I claimed we were looking too high up," said Curt, "but now I believe we are settling too low."

"Where do you think Hank Night spent the winters?" asked Lawless, scribbling on the notepad.

105

"What does where he put down his keel have to do with the murder of Jersey Zayres?" demanded Clement.

Lawless seemed to be ignoring the pushy detective, but Curt surmised Clement's stale coffee breath, which seemed to permeate the general vicinity, was keeping her at bay. She tapped her blue Flair Pen on the report and said, "Says here that prior to discovering Hank Night in the cellar, the owner of Yellow Umbrella Books ran into Hank Night in the parking lot behind the bookstore."

Clement snorted. "That fish bait was seen everywhere on the Cape. Why, last fall, he got nabbed riding the Hyannis Dinner Train. Security tossed his sorry butt off just south of downtown Sandwich."

Lawless ran the blue Flair across her bottom lip, back and forth, thinking out loud, "Last time the bookstore owner saw Night was the previous afternoon...hmm. It's logical to assume that Hank Night rode out storms and winters in the cellar of Yellow Umbrella Books." Her green eyes zeroed in on Curt.

"I dare say, the ol' boy may have been among the ghosts that rumors claim are haunting that dank and musty crypt," said Curt, tongue in cheek. The silence that followed triggered him to look into the stunned eyes of Lawless and Clement.

"My apologies," blustered Curt. "My remark was made in poor taste."

"What's going on?" asked Robert Pomoroy, strolling into the room.

Lawless shifted her focus onto the young Fed entering the room. She looked back at Curt and then looked down at the paperwork. "According to the death certificate," she said, "Hank Night likely succumbed to the toxic effect of fentanyl, cocaine, and..." She gawked at Curt. "Drain cleaner?"

"The connection between Hank Night and Jersey Zayres is obvious," said Clement. "Night, the addict; and Zayres, the supplier. They met on the loading dock and came to blows over price, which is motive. Night shoved Zayres, which is the means. Zayres ends up in the dumpster, impaled with a metal corner protector. No matter how you look at it, this is a case of out-and-out murder."

Again, Lawless ignored the detective. "Fentanyl is thirty to fifty times more powerful than heroin. End-stage cancer patients are given fentanyl via patches."

"That is correct," said Curt. "Patients whose brains have become resistant to ongoing painkiller therapy are prescribed fentanyl, which fits into nerve receptors in the brain, which blocks the sensation of pain. Brains of drug abusers react the same way after taking Vicodin and codeine, not realizing that a similar amount of fentanyl has lethal consequences, blocking nerves that tell the lungs to keep breathing, depriving the brain of oxygen with the end result of the heart stopping."

"A silent subdued way to go," commented Robert Pomoroy.

"Indeed," said Curt, giving a nod to the young Fed.

"Which explains why Hank Night was in the bookstore cellar all that time, dying, and nobody heard a thing," said Pomoroy, returning the nod.

Clement grunted. "Not until that fish bait stunk up the place."

"Rodney, please," said Curt.

Lawless heaved a sigh. "Drug abusers should think twice about fentanyl."

"I express little optimism that overall drug behavior will ever change," said Curt.

"If it isn't one drug, it'll be another," grumbled Clement. "New drugs and cocktails are being cooked up in kitchens across this country—and across the world—every single day."

"Substance abuse is a human condition that has been a mainstay since Henry was a pup," said Curt. "An eternal plague to humanity."

"Sixty percent of drug deaths involve combinations of illegal substances," said Pomoroy.

"Which begs the question: Where did Jersey Zayres get the fentanyl?" asked Lawless, looking up at Clement. Her gaze shifted to Pomoroy and then to Curt. Suddenly, dawn spread across her face. "At the Rehab Center... Jersey Zayres got the fentanyl at the Rehab Center."

Curt remained mum.

She glanced at Clement.

The detective sent Pomoroy a surreptitious glimpse.

Her eyelids tightened into slits as she focused on the young Fed.

Appearing to be completely at ease, Pomoroy said, "Reporting your suspicions, Ms. Lawless, will jeopardize an ongoing investigation."

"It is news," she countered.

"It is," agreed Pomoroy. He looked her square in the eyes. "Will you agree that drug abuse on the Cape is a problem?"

"It is everywhere," she said.

Pomoroy persisted, "Not only with overdose deaths, but also associated injuries and deaths of innocent people resulting from DUI accidents, fires, violence, etcetera?"

"I agree," said Lawless, moving her focus onto the police report in her hand.

"And as a citizen of Chatham and Cape Cod, you would like to see some solution to the problem."

This time, Lawless remained mum.

"You've had some sort of personal experience in the matter, haven't you?" said Pomoroy.

Again, no response. However, she did look up at the young Fed. Her eyes did meet his.

Pomoroy didn't flinch.

Moments crawled.

Curt sensed that the reporter could have drilled the toe of her one-inch heel into Pomoroy's groin; even then the young Fed would not have flinched.

Clement intervened: "Okay, okay. Have it your way, Lawless."

From the way she seemed to sag, she was clearly relieved and grateful to have gotten first dibs on a story that as yet no other reporter had even gotten wind of.

"But listen," spoke up Pomoroy.

Lawless straightened, her eyes rounded on the Fed.

"Before reporting your suspicions," said Pomoroy, "at least give the investigation a little more time."

She tapped the blue Flair Pen on her right cheek. "How much is a little?"

"Not much."

"In this cynical day and age, a little time can be priceless," said Lawless.

Pomoroy got the hint.

Curt got the hint.

So did Clement. "Look, lady. Drugs may still be oozing out of that Rehab Center. With Zayres dead and Pearle Key still on the run, we have no idea if the leak is plugged or not. At this point, we are so stumped it stinks worse than Hank Night in the cellar of that bookstore. I'd consider I'd owe you big time if you'd hold off on any story relating to the Rehab Center."

Her eyes narrowed on the detective. "Give me a front row seat?"

"When I know something concrete," said Clement, "so will you."

She glanced at Pomoroy and received a nearly indiscernible nod.

SEPTEMBER 15 – NOON

HIGHLAND BEACH

North of the Highland Light, monarch butterflies flitted in the sun, southbound on the seventy-degree breeze. Crickets chirped urgently, aware of decreasing daylight and temperatures of this level occurring less often, both of which portended eminent demise. Summer crowds had evaporated, leaving the beach remarkably tranquil. At water's edge, sandpipers skittered beneath the perfect blue sky. There was not the slightest omen of the hurricane arcing toward the Cape from the southeast, offering nothing of the storm swells about to ravage the coastline, engraving the sands and depositing driftwood and empty shells for autumn tourists, offering nothing of the graphic ocean soundscape to come.

Jenny and Dan were meandering along the outer dunes fringed with grasses that were now the color of straw. Hands clasped, their arms swung in metered time with each returning wave. Pant legs and shirtsleeves were rolled up. Windbreakers were tied to their waists.

At a tidal cutaway, Jenny and Dan stopped and exchanged an extended kiss. Her vanilla perfume delighted his nostrils. "M-m-m," he murmured.

She raised her face.

He licked beneath her chin.

They fell back into the sand. Heated necking ensued.

Dan reached into his pocket, his fingers hunting for the last two hits he had scored from the late Jersey Zayres.

He didn't know each and every one of the substances contained in the hit, but Jersey Zayres bragged the concoction was the best ever. Dan had no idea that a portion of the concoction originated from the Rehab Center. What he did know is that these two hits were the last he— or anybody else—was ever going to score from the iced drug dealer. Therefore, Dan was intending to have one last real good time until he could score again from whoever eventually took over the drug trade on the Cape.

"Hey, what's that?" shrieked Jenny.

Spasms of terror sickened Dan as he rolled away from her. *Don't tell me her husband's tracked us down already,* he thought. Scanning the beach, he stuffed the two hits deep into his pocket. Sandpipers, gulls, and in the distance, a hang glider attempting a liftoff behind a high-speed boat. Dan gave a nervous chuckle. "Sure wish I could do that."

Jenny sent him a strange look then her eyes followed his line of sight. "Not that glider guy. Over there, Dan. See? Something is in the water!"

He scanned the incoming tide. "I don't see anything." He reached out for her, his hormones swelling, just missing her shirttail as she jumped to her feet. He fell back on his elbows, his lips pursed. He leered at her slapping the sand off her hands. Reluctantly, he got to his feet. *Put this garbage to rest—real quick like,* he told himself, *and then get back to the fine art of fornication.*

"You must see it now," she insisted.

He squinted at an object rising and falling with the waves. "Yeah, I see it."

"Do you think it's a whale?" she asked.

He rubbed his hands across the front of his shirt, trying to quell his hormones. "Could be..." Time and again, the object sank into the churn and then resurfaced. "A small whale, if it is a whale."

Jenny shielded her eyes from the sun's glare and walked down to water's edge. "Maybe it's a lobster pot that's come loose."

"Or a bait tub from a fishing boat," said Dan. Catching up to her, he snagged her hand, intent on pulling her around, taking her in his arms, and...

She yanked her hand away and hooked both hands on her hips, staring at the object. Her voice faltered. "I-I don't think so." Her hands suddenly grasped her cheeks as her eyes bugged out.

Dan squinted at the object. His heart skipped a beat. "That is a person!"

Summer And August

SEPTEMBER 15 – MIDNIGHT

THE KEY RESIDENCE

"Stop it, Quincy," Beverly whimpered, rejecting the beam of the penlight zigzagging, blinking on and off, across her bedroom wall. "Don't think for one minute I am going to answer you, so just stop it! How your signal even made it through this hurricane is…a…a miracle. A miracle, Quincy. Today was anything but a miracle."

Beverly felt as though her childhood playmate and confidant—ex confidant—was there with her in her bedroom. "You haven't spoken two words to me since somebody killed Jersey. Why? Not even now? Now that Mom's dead? All you can do is signal? You know they found her, Quincy—don't tell me you don't!"

She squeezed her eyelids closed and yanked the pink patchwork quilt over her head. "You know better than to even think Mom could kill anybody!"

Lightning snapped. Thunder exploded. The entire cottage rattled. At times, Beverly thought the hurricane slamming into the elbow of Cape Cod might blow the entire world away. At times, she wished it would.

The tropical warmth that fueled the storm eluded her. She got colder with every broken heartbeat. Shivering head to toe, she reached out for her extra pillow, dragged it under the quilt, and hugged it.

"Don't worry about me, Quincy. Bobby is downstairs. He takes good care of me, you know. Funny how he has been here for me and not you." She pursed her lips, fed-up, frustrated, down-in-the-dumps. "I didn't want to be alone tonight, Quincy. Bobby knew that. I didn't even have to tell him. He even put me to bed, pulled the blankets up to my chin, tucked the blankets around me."

She recalled how Bobby pushed her hair back then kissed her lightly on the mouth. His spicy strength filled her senses. Without thinking, she wrapped her arms around his waist and kissed him back. When he tried to pull away, she held on tight, whispering, "Don't go. Please?"

He put his cheek against her temple, his warm breath drifting past her ear. His voice was soft, lingering, "There's no place else I'd rather be."

"Then stay."

"Only if you try to get some rest."

"Rest," she whispered, staring up at the ceiling lit up by flashes of lightning. "I don't know what rest is anymore."

Bobby laughed a small laugh then broke away. "I'll be downstairs."

"Promise?"

"Promise," he said.

At the bedroom door, Bobby switched off the light. Beverly could see his silhouette against the dim light that filtered up the stairway. And then he was gone.

She tried to sleep, but it was impossible because the penlight started flashing on the wall and kept flashing. "Stop it, Quincy."

Then those vivid images of the afternoon kept careening through her mind, howling louder than the wind flailing the cottage. She and Bobby were in the Viper, zooming up Route 6, ahead of them, the tail lights of a car driven by Debra Lawless, a reporter Bobby knew. He said Debra wasn't pushy. Debra was fair, levelheaded—even though he thought that Debra might be hard-pressed not to give away her next book contract in exchange for an exclusive.

"An exclusive on what?" Beverly asked.

Bobby frowned at her and then back at the tail lights. He never did answer the question.

Highland Beach wasn't that far, but to Beverly, it seemed a million miles away. Her mind was a jumbled mass: *What if the person on the beach is Mom? What if it isn't? And if it is Mom, how did she end up on that beach? Mom is a rotten swimmer—and she hates boats. She only tolerates boats and water long enough to get to Monomoy Island and then when she gets there, she won't even dunk her toes. Aggravates Aunt Celia to no end. And if the weather and waves aren't right to begin with, Mom absolutely refuses to set foot in a boat. Lately, storms have riled up the ocean and now another hurricane is coming. No, it can't be Mom. It just can't be.*

The Highland Light passed on her right. She and Quincy had gone there on a third grade field trip. *It's the oldest lighthouse on the Cape—established in 1798. At sixty-six feet tall, its light can be seen by transatlantic sailors and... What am I doing thinking about that stuff at a time like this?*

Beverly thought of the many nights coming back from Provincetown, Celia Beale driving, Pearle Key in the front passenger-seat, she and Quincy craning their necks all the way to Truro to see the lighthouse's white light flashing every five seconds.

She blinked—and Bobby was pulling up to Highland Beach. She gawked at the circular crowd that had gathered close to the roiling surf, the geysers of chalky foam, and the nauseatingly purple cloudbanks. Whitecaps rode the building waves that crested and formed huge hands that smacked down on the sand with earth-shaking force, drenching the sand, and then snatching up pieces of beach—as if kidnappers stealing away innocents, dragging them into the dark void beneath the turbulent sea.

Bobby was opening her door. His hand was warm and gentle as he took hers. "Everything's going to be okay, Bev."

She was on her feet, clumsy, brittle, sinking ankle-deep into the sand.

His arm encircled her waist as Bobby introduced Beverly to Debra Lawless. The reporter's pink lips moved, but her voice was drowned out by a burly male reporter, microphone in hand, hollering, "Miss Key! A moment, please, Miss Key! Do you think the body down there on the beach is your mother? Do you think she was murdered? Could she have committed suicide? Was your mother suicidal, Miss Key? If so, why? What put her over the edge?"

"Back off, Mac!" barked a female voice—Beverly sensed the voice belonged to Debra Lawless.

One step. Another. The erratic salty gale picked up sodden clumps of sand and debris and flung them full force at Beverly, scouring her face and whipping through her hair. It was hard to see, hard to walk forward.

Half the crowd split in the middle and then yawned open like a double gate.

Beverly stopped, her mind trying to process the waterlogged body, lying flat, stretched across soggy sand. Mutilated. Drained of color. Caked in filth and seaweed.

"Is this your mother, Miss Key?" demanded the burly reporter, pressing closer and closer.

Beverly gave him a blank stare. "I-I…"

"Is this the long-missing Pearle Key?" bullied the burly reporter.

Bobby got in his face. "I am not going to tell you to back off more than once!" His frame was no match for the burly reporter. Still, the burly reporter backed off.

Leaning her cheek against Bobby's chest, Beverly peered out of the corner of her eye at the mutilated body. "Gray hair. That's not Mom."

118

A giant wave crested and then bombarded the sand; only yards away, but still, the burly reporter's voice came through loud and clear, "If this is not Pearle Key then who is this? Where is Pearle Key? Hank Night confessed to killing Jersey Zayres on his deathbed, so what's stopping Pearle Key from showing herself?"

Debra and Bobby put their backs to the burly reporter, shielding Beverly.

Months of anxiety swamped Beverly. She focused in and out on the body. Suddenly, her heart knotted into a fist. "That blouse..." She lifted her head off Bobby's chest to get a better view. "It looks...familiar...so terribly...familiar..."

Beverly clamped her eyes shut, trembling in her bed. Yet she could still see the cotton eyelet fabric, discolored, rotted by time, salinity, and sand. Yet she could still see the missing buttons, the stitching at the sleeves, which could only mean that the blouse was sleeveless. "Mom's favorite blouse. I bought it for her last year in Chatham."

She buried her face into Bobby's chest and sobbed. "Mom always said she loved that blouse, because it doesn't show through her pink scrubs. Pink. The color of hope. But here she is, Bobby. Dead! Mom is dead!" She felt herself faint away. Bobby caught her up in his arms and took her away from there, away from that crowd, away from...

"...Away from Mom." If Beverly hadn't been lying in bed at this moment, she would have collapsed on the floor. "Oh, Mom, how in the world did you end up like that?"

Lightning lit up the bedroom.

Suddenly her eyes bugged out. She swore she was on the beach again, focusing in and out on the body. A voice in her head was shrieking, *"Gray hair! The ocean washed out all the henna! The ends are the same ugly, off-color as..."*

She bolted upright, tremors wracking her. "The same color as mine!" She wrestled with the bedcovers that stuck to her like a shroud.

119

Free at last, she dropped her feet over the edge of the bed and stared at the beam of the penlight zigzagging across the wall, blinking, on and off. "Stop it Quincy!" she cried. She wrapped her arms around herself. "You and I know Mom didn't kill your precious Jersey. We both know she could never do a thing like that."

Beverly slid her feet into her slippers then glared at the penlight beam. "So tell me why, Quincy. Why is Mom dead? That's what I want to know." She pursed her lips against the flow of tears. "Why, Quincy? Tell me why?"

She mopped her hand across her runny nose and stood up. She adjusted her pajamas then grabbed her robe off the footboard of the bed. Stuffing her arms into the sleeves, she left her bedroom. She stopped in the hallway, cinching the belt and squinting into Pearle's bedroom. *Mom's never going to sleep in that bed again.*

She choked back grief, fear, and the feeling that she was about to shatter into a million pieces. *Nobody will ever love me in that same unselfish, unconditional way you did, Mom. You always put me first—and I took you for granted. I'm so sorry. I didn't know you were going to die. If only I'd known...*

She heard a noise. Her mind picked it apart as she glanced over her shoulder. "Quincy? Is that you? Did you say, 'Get a grip'?"

Lightning. Thunder. A penlight flash.

A chill shot through Beverly. "Get a grip. Of course, Quincy isn't here. His penlight is still flashing on my bedroom wall, so he's in his bedroom window." She hooked her chin. "Of course, you're not here. You are never here for me anymore."

Pursing her lips, she wobbled down the stairs. At the bottom, she peered around the corner. She seemed to melt at the sight of Bobby sitting in the recliner he had pulled up in front of the sliding glass door. Even though he faced away from her, she knew he was awake. And then she heard him humming. "*Go Ask Alice.* He's humming, *Go Ask Alice*? Why is he...?"

His hand swung out from the chair and reached out to her.

She swiveled toward the stairs, bent on running away; but then she stopped. She shivered then turned around and took several steps toward him. Emotions jumbled her insides and she began to whimper, "Mom's dead, Bobby. Why? How did that happen to her?"

"I'm trying to figure that out, Bev."

"Mom didn't kill herself, did she? That mean reporter shouldn't have even suggested that Mom could have done a thing like that. She hated water—and boats. She was murdered, Bobby; that's how she ended up in the water and on that beach. But why would anybody murder Mom? And..."

His hand beckoned.

She hesitated, sick with grief, gazing at his outstretched hand. Comfort was there—with Bobby— safety, warmth...

"Come sit with me, Bev."

She wobbled across the room and put her hand in his. He pulled her around to the front of the recliner and then onto his lap. As his arms enfolded her, his warmth radiated through her. She went limp against him, whispering against his neck, "What am I going to do now?"

His cheek stroked her forehead. "Everything's going to be okay, Bev."

"You won't leave me, will you, Bobby?"

"Never."

She looked into his maple syrup eyes.

"Never," he said, squeezing her close to him.

She rested her head on his shoulder and stared out beyond the glass, beyond the patio and into the night beset by a tempest hell-bent on destruction. Beneath her palm resting on Bobby's chest, his heart beat steady. His chest rose and fell, slow, steady. Her breath aligned with his, steady. *Get a grip* weaved through her mind as her eyelids drooped.

SEPTEMBER 16 – 7:30 A.M.
THE BEALE RESIDENCE

"What are you doing home, honey?"

Quincy ignored Celia, but he knew she was standing in the doorway. He felt her eyes tracking him as he yanked clothes out of his bureau.

"Were classes canceled today?"

"No, Ma," he snapped while stuffing the clothes into a backpack.

Only moments before, the Viper parked in the driveway next door had stopped Quincy in his tracks. The image of that snazzy car and what it meant dominated his thinking: *Pomoroy stayed the night! Beverly gave in to that smooth-talker! How could she? Now, she's lost to me, forever!* Quincy took a step back. *I didn't realize so much resentment was bottled up inside me.* He shook his head side-to-side. *Get a grip, man.* But then the images came back with a vengeance. His insides knotted. *I must've looked like such a fool to them, last night, me flashing that penlight into her window!* His jaw clenched at the image of Beverly and Pomoroy lying in her bed; *Laughing at me!*

Celia took hold of his sleeve. She gave a tug. Another.

He swiveled, jouncing his hands. "What, Ma?"

She grabbed his arms. "Didn't you hear me?" She shook him. "I asked you three times, 'Where are you going?'"

His forearms came up and brushed her off. "I'm going nuts—that's where!"

Shock riddled her face. "Going nuts?"

Quincy huffed. "I need to get out of here, right now!"

"But where are you going to go?"

"Far, far away!"

She stumbled backward. "Far away?" She caught her balance. "But, honey, I don't understand."

Quincy rammed the drawer closed and yanked open another one. He smelled his own sweat. The shower he had taken an hour ago meant nothing now. He snagged deodorant, aftershave, and other grooming supplies and stuffed them into the backpack.

"Please, tell me what's wrong."

In the mirror, he saw her palms reaching out to him. "Honey?"

His lips clamped together like a vise as his insides exploded, *Don't touch me!* He closed his eyes. *And quit whining! Can't stand it when you whine! You've been doing way too much of it lately!*

Yet Quincy couldn't bring himself to be mean to Celia. He let his head drop back. *Why can't I just tell her what I think?*

He filled his lungs with air and shook off frustration. He straightened then looked into the mirror, square into her eyes. "I can't stand any more garbage," he said. "The Cape. Aunt Pearle turning up on the beach like that, the way..." His eyes met his own staring back at him in the mirror.

If only I could open my mouth and say what I really want to say, he thought. *Say that I hate the way Pomoroy hangs around, comforting Beverly—the way I want to. If only I could say I love Beverly right to her face! Now, on top of everything else, that conniving pretender spent the night with the girl I love.*

Quincy turned to Celia. Panic had stolen the color from her face. Her eyes were zipping side-to-side, alarmed,

124

like those of a criminal about to get caught. He felt like a heel. "I-I just need to get away, Ma. Far, far away."

She stood there, wringing her hands. All of a sudden, her dark eyebrows fused and her arms dropped to her sides. Her hands scraped together as she turned and stepped to the window.

She's going to see the Viper in Beverly's driveway, Quincy thought. *She's going to know I never even got to my truck before I saw Bobby's car and then like a sniveling weenie, I hauled butt back into the house. Yup, she sees it. And now look. She's grinding her teeth the way she always does when something's got her all pissed off. No doubt about it, she's reached the same conclusion I did: Bobby stayed over last night.*

Celia spun around, those black eyes of hers impaling Quincy. For a moment, he worried that she might kill him.

Her eyes softened. Her voice changed, too. It came out sticky sweet. "You know what, honey? I think getting away is not really such a bad idea at all."

His jaw dropped.

She smiled and nodded pensively. "Yes. I have been thinking the same thing lately. What a coincidence."

"Really, Ma?"

"My sweet baby boy. From the instant I set eyes on you, I loved you. You know that. I only want what's best for you, honey." She laughed—a low, dreadfully, ugly laugh. "And what's best for me, of course."

He eyed her. The look on her face would have turned the devil to stone. "You're going nuts, Ma. Just like I am."

She turned her back to him. "You need a new start, honey. Simple as that." She rolled her shoulders. "So do I." She sucked in a deep breath. "I think we should go someplace where we can get real peace of mind." She looked back at him, her dark eyebrows high on her forehead. "So now what, honey?"

"Geez, Ma, I don't have a clue."

Under her breath, she said something; something along the lines of, "You never did have a clue."

"What did you say, Ma?"

"Sell the house!" she exclaimed. "Of course! I will put it up for sale tomorrow!"

He frowned at her. "But Ma, where are we going to live after we sell it?"

"How about North Carolina? Or maybe Florida?"

He gave a tentative nod then ventured, "Well, California might be…"

"California!" she cried. "What a great idea, honey! But you know what? We don't have to stay in the United States. I hear Italy is nice—cheap living, too; lots to do. Germany's kind of expensive."

"I'm sure I can transfer all my college credits anywhere we go," he said.

"So, what do you think, honey? We going to do this or what?"

Quincy stood there, stunned.

"California it is then!" she exclaimed.

All sense of urgency had drained out of Quincy quicker than water circling a washbasin at warp speed. "Uhm…guess we have to make plans… Do some research on the Internet…"

She gazed at him, completely at ease. "We can hop around if you like, honey; try a few places as we head out west. But only for a little while. You know very well that I don't have a lot of money. We'd've been just fine if those nasty cops would have just closed the murder case and handed over Jersey's things to me. Uhm… I mean… Handed Jersey's things over to *us*."

SEPTEMBER 16 – 9:00 A.M.

THE KEY RESIDENCE

"Are you sure you're going to be alright?" Bobby asked as his hand gripped the doorknob.

Beverly clamped her hands together, feeling scared and lost.

He glanced over his shoulder at her.

She looked back at the recliner where she had spent the night curled up in his arms. It was still facing out at the deck and the grassy patch of a backyard that dissolved into a restless ocean. The Suncatchers attached to the glass were spreading rainbows shimmering across the floor, walls and ceiling. It all seemed sacrilegious given the gruesome discovery of Pearle Key's body washed up on the beach north of the Highland Lighthouse.

"I can take another day off if you want me to," Bobby offered.

She turned to him. He was facing her now. His hard-as-nails muscles bulged beneath the sleeves of his faded blue denim shirt that gaped open in the front. A slice of the holster strap was unmistakable against his white strappy T-shirt, but to Bobby—and everybody who knew him—the holster and gun were just ordinary articles of clothing. She gazed into his maple syrup eyes. "I don't want you to leave—and I know you don't want to either...but...you're never going to find out who murdered Mom and catch the guy if you don't go to work."

He let go of the doorknob and stepped over to her. His hands cupped her cheeks then pulled her face to his. His kiss was soft and gentle.

Her heart cried out, *"Tell him you love him!"*

He loves me, she thought. *I know he does. But what if we don't love each other? I mean* really *love each other? What if what I'm feeling is vulnerability, a result of months of stress and now grief? What if what Bobby is feeling is only manliness, the need to protect? How does a person take back I love you?*

"Bev?"

She whispered in his mouth, "You better go."

He pulled back. "Yeah." He took his car keys out of the right pocket of his blue jeans. "There's too much to do that can't get done until the investigation is over and done with and the coroner's office releases…"

She hung her head.

"I'll do everything I can to speed things up."

"I know you will," she said, looking up at him.

He swiveled toward the kitchen door. "Call me on my cell phone—anytime."

She gazed at him.

He glanced over his shoulder at her and smiled. "I'll pick up—no matter what I'm doing."

She nodded.

His head tilted to one side. "We'll go for a run on the beach when I get back."

She smiled a thin smile. "Go, Bobby."

His hand gripped the door handle. This time, he opened the door.

She followed him out of the cottage and halfway to his car. She watched him get in. The motor rumbled to life. The window whirred down then his hand came out, waving to her. She waved back, feeling like a little girl—as if she were seeing her father off to work. *If only Mom had told me* who my father is. I always thought a day would come that she would. I could've gotten her to tell me, I just know it. If only I had more time. If only...

The Viper backed up, turned out onto the road, and then stopped. Bobby waved again.

So did she.

Tires spun and the Viper sped off.

She was alone. So all alone.

Silent moments devoid of thought passed. The breeze fanned her face. She felt like a soap bubble floating along. How far was this breeze called life going to take her before she popped? She would not care at all—if it weren't for Bobby.

A familiar sound reached her ears. *Was that the gate?* She turned. Strands of her hair grazed her face. She brushed them aside. *Is that... Get a grip, I'm just seeing things. But it is. It's Aunt Celia. She's actually coming through that gate. What does she want? She's got a lot of nerve to come over here after snubbing me all this time.* A chill raced through Beverly. *Was she waiting for Bobby to leave before coming over here? She's not exactly smiling, although she does have a fairly pleasant look on her face, appropriate considering Mom is...*

"My sweet little Beverly," whined Celia, opening her arms. "I am so devastated."

Beverly dropped her hands to her sides. Finding herself wrapped in Celia's arms, she didn't not know what to think, what to feel.

"Things cannot go on like they have been any longer, sweetie. Our dear Pearle would not have wanted it this way."

Beverly stood there, angry, hurt, and also devastated. Formulating words seemed impossible.

"And my poor baby boy." Celia held Beverly at arm's length. Her dark eyes penetrated Beverly. "He has just been beside himself. And it's all my fault, sweetie. I really must make things right between you two."

"I-I don't know what to say," Beverly stammered.

"You don't need to say a thing, sweetie," said Celia, taking Beverly by the hand. "Come on. I'll make us a cup of tea and we can talk."

Beverly broke away. "I need to take a shower."

"Oh, don't be silly," said Celia as a hint of annoyance crept across her face. "I have seen you dirty lots of times." She snagged Beverly's hand. "Yup, children and dirt go hand in hand."

Beverly tried to pull away. "No, really. I can't. I…"

"Of course, you can, sweetie," said Celia, not quite seething.

"Please, Aunt Celia," whimpered Beverly. "I'm really not up to it."

Deaf to all protests, Celia towed Beverly through the gate and into the Beale cottage. She pulled out a kitchen chair. "Here now, sweetie, sit down and relax."

Beverly sagged onto the chair.

Celia marched over to the stove and lit the gas flame under the teapot. "Quincy is off to classes," she said, taking two teacups out of the cupboard. "After he left, I went over to the A&P and bought a dozen of his favorite cinnamon buns. Won't he be surprised when he gets back? They smell so good. Cinnamon donuts are your favorite, too, aren't they, sweetie?"

Beverly attempted to nod and wave her head no at the same time. "I'm not really hungry."

Celia stepped over to the table and patted Beverly's hand. "You have to eat, sweetie. Pearle would not have liked how thin you have gotten these last months."

"Somehow, I have to get through a few more," said Beverly.

"You will, sweetie," said Celia, as the teapot began to whistle.

"If bad things don't stop happening—and soon," Beverly said, "I'm going to lose my mind."

One side of Celia's face twitched. "Things are going to be just fine."

Celia stepped back to the stove and turned off the gas. The whistling died down as she reached for the ceramic canister on the shelf. "You take milk in your tea, right, sweetie?"

Beverly stared at the canister that was shaped like a killer whale. The lid was its head. Like a fishnet, Celia's hands came down on the canister. One hand ripped off the head while the other invaded its gut and seized two teabags.

"I take lemon myself," Celia said, replacing the lid. She removed the wrappers from the teabags then holding the tags, dropped the bags into the cups. "I've been so dreadful to you and Quincy." She draped the tags over the rims of the cups. "You don't know how much I have been thinking about it." She snagged the teapot and poured steaming water over the teabags. "I just have to set things right. Pearle always wanted things right." She placed the teapot onto the stove then picked up the teacups and brought them to the table. "I don't have to tell you how hard these last few months have been." She set one cup in front of Beverly and the other on the table in front of the next empty chair. "It's just so hard to know who to trust these days." She sat down and dipped her teabag several times as if waiting for a fish to bite.

Beverly made no move toward the cup. Celia forgot about the milk anyway—and also, the lemon.

Celia took a sip of tea then took a wistful breath. "I still can't believe the FBI thinks our dear Pearle was stealing drugs from the Rehab Center."

Beverly shot a look at Celia. "Stealing drugs? Mom?"

"Can you imagine?" said Celia, staring off into space and shaking her head. "How can anybody ever think such a thing of our darling Pearle?" Celia took a sip of tea then put down her cup. Her dark eyes locked on Beverly. "I know I'm a little rough around the edges, sweetie, but Pearle was different. She was such a pussycat. That poor woman wouldn't take a nickel off the sidewalk. Everybody knows that. How can the FBI even conceive of your adorable mother doing a thing like that? I'm sure Bobby told you about..."

"No, Bobby didn't tell me," cut in Beverly. Anger bubbled to the surface, blinding her to the devious surprise slithering across Celia's face.

"The investigation at the Rehab Center isn't news, sweetie," said Celia, avoiding eye contact.

"I know, I know, but Bobby..."

"He didn't tell you his investigation was focused on our Pearle?" Celia raised an eyebrow. She appeared thoroughly appalled as she eyed Beverly. "Come on, now. Are you absolutely sure Bobby didn't tell you?"

Beverly jumped to her feet. "Don't you think I'd remember a thing like that?"

Celia cocked her head to one side. "Oh, dear, I..." She peered down at her teacup, she heaved a sigh. "Listen, sweetie, I think you really should know..."

"Know what?"

Celia waved her head side to side. "Talk to Bobby about it."

"No! You tell me!"

A slight twitch rippled the left side of Celia's mouth. She cleared her throat then said, "Bobby and his cop friends are about to nail our poor innocent Pearle for heading all the drug trafficking activity at the Rehab Center."

SEPTEMBER 16 – 6:00 P.M.

THE SHIRLINGTON RESIDENCE

Curt slid out of the Envoy, leaving his briefcase and navy blue suit jacket on the front passenger-side seat. As he headed to the veranda that encircled his home, his right hand pressed the remote button that locked the doors while his left hand loosened his J. Garcia tie. He paused on the top step and took in the sight of his slender, five-foot-two wife sitting in one of the white rocking chairs, their son at her breast. A swirl of spice-colored hair draped her right shoulder.

Her toffee-colored eyes met his. Then her hand reached out to him.

He smiled and stepped over to her. He took her hand then bent and kissed her forehead. He inhaled her jasmine perfume. "Thank goodness for you and this veranda," he said.

"And J. C.," she added.

He squeezed her hand. "And Jeffrey Curtis."

"Another long day," she said, not asking. She already knew it.

He kissed the infant on the forehead then straightened. With one finger, he caressed the miniature cheek. "This day was enough to give the sanest of blokes a lifetime of lurid nightmares," he said.

"Time to let it go," she said.

"Indeed," said Curt.

He stepped over to the screen door and pulled it open. As the door closed behind him, he rolled up the sleeves of his white shirt.

The pungent odor of tomato sauce spiked with oregano, garlic, and basil, tickled his nostrils. *Ah, Emma LaRosa—God rest your soul—you mentored so many great cooks.*

His stomach let him know its sad state of emptiness, but his brain stopped him from disturbing Penny and Jeffrey Curtis. *The very moment I even think about going to the kitchen to fix myself something to eat, she intercedes. Of late, she has become such a mother hen—not that I don't like that...*

At the bar, he mixed a Rob Roy in an old-fashioned glass, mulling over the autopsy he performed that day on the remains of Pearle Key. "A bit dodgy to say the least— more so knowing a family member. An extended period of time at sea left the corpse an atrocious catastrophe: decomposed; exsanguinated; fish bait; caught in the tide; banged against rocks; butchered then inundated with sand and beach debris. Tsk, tsk, tsk."

He returned to the veranda and stood at the railing, massaging the old-fashioned glass, now only half-full of Rob Roy.

"Tell me about the autopsy," said Penny, rocking the slumbering infant.

Curt took a cleansing breath. The alcohol was slowly putting him at ease. "You don't want to know."

"Sure I do."

He propped his left black loafer on the railing. After a moment, he said, "Bottom line is: blood and tissue samples reveal fentanyl, cocaine, and several other illegal substances—one being pancuronium bromide, which remains identifiable for many months in cadavers—the very same cocktail that contributed to Hank Night's death, poor sod."

"Drain cleaner sped up the process," said Penny.

"Aye. In the case of Pearle Key, add strangulation—hyoid bones were crushed—and a triple dose of that cocktail."

Penny winced. "Somebody really had it in for her."

"Takes care of the theory that Pearle Key murdered Jersey Zayres then killed herself out of guilt," said Curt. He took a sip of Rob Roy.

"Poor Beverly has been through enough," said Penny. "She doesn't need people thinking that way."

Curt took a moment to watch the copper Viper pull up behind the Envoy. Then he said, "By and large, I am quite pleased to have ruled out suicide." He chugged the last of his drink then removed his foot from the railing. "As you say, the lass does not deserve such misery." He stepped over to the white rocking chair next to Penny and J.C. and then sat down. He scraped the bottom of the empty old-fashion glass up and down the arm of the rocking chair. "I have no inkling as to how or why or if fatigue is muddling my reasoning; nevertheless, I am of the mind that Hank fortuitously came across the murder scene at the dumpster; which is how the ol' boy got his hands on the lethal cocktail and valuables belonging to Jersey Zayres."

"Could be Hank was on that loading dock to complete a previous scheduled drug deal," suggested Pomoroy, stepping up onto the veranda.

Penny smiled up at the young Fed. "Where's Beverly?"

A pained look riddled his face. He sagged on the railing. "She's mad at me—real mad."

Penny stopped rocking. "For what?"

Pomoroy hesitated. He crossed his arms. "She found out about the Rehab investigation and that Pearle Key is suspected of being involved with it."

"It was inevitable, Robert," said Curt, noting the young Fed's scruffy appearance.

"Yeah," said Pomoroy. "I really intended to tell her about everything—myself—when the time was right."

"But the right time never came, huh?" said Penny, once again rocking J.C.

Pomoroy ran his hand through his matted hair. "There's always something tearing Beverly apart. It never stops. I just didn't have the heart to give her more to freak out about."

"Most of all, you were afraid she'd react just like this," said Penny.

Pomoroy pulled back the side of his mouth and clicked. His face took on a remote appearance as if he wasn't standing on the veranda with them. He turned and looked out over the lawn.

"And now she won't even answer her cell phone when you call her," said Penny.

His shoulders heaved as the young Fed took in an all-encompassing sigh.

"I'll talk to her," said Penny.

Pomoroy sent a thank-you look over his right shoulder and then looked out over the lawn again.

After several moments of silence, Curt spoke up, "Refresh my memory if you will, Robert, concerning the cameras outside the Chatham Inn on the day of Jersey Zayres death. I cannot recall several of the details revealed on them."

"Zayres arrived in his Caddie," said Pomoroy. "The point of a gun—silencer attached to it—poked out the driver's side window and went off. The camera went blank. Next camera picked him up. Same thing. Happened every time to every camera: Jersey is there; gun fires; cameras go out. Nobody heard one single gunshot. Nobody heard or saw a thing." His jaw tightened. "So what else is new? It's no surprise that Zayres would have used a silencer. Obviously, he didn't want witnesses to see what was about to go down."

"Or who else was coming or going," added Penny.

"We know Hank Night was there working," said Pomoroy.

"As was I," said Curt.

Pomoroy gave Curt the hairy eyeball. "Don't start with that again. You are so far above suspicion that even the angels can't get a bead on you."

Curt shrugged. "Nevertheless, I cannot get beyond the old boy confessing to the murder of Jersey Zayres. Most assuredly, Hank acted like a sturdy individual, but as a physician, I saw through the façade. I am quite sure that he had all he could do to get himself down into that dumpster and clamber around for the goods, never mind getting himself out afterward."

"And among those goods was the gun you found at the Yellow Umbrella," said Pomoroy.

"By all rights, deathbed confessions hold up in the court of public opinion," said Penny.

"Debra Lawless will attest to that," said Pomoroy.

Curt stood up then stepped to the railing beside Pomoroy. Bracing on elbows, he clasped his hands then gazed out over the lawn with the young Fed. "A deep-seeded suspicion haunts me and the more I mull it over, the more I am convinced that the murder of Pearle Key and Hank's overdose death has to be related to the murder of Jersey Zayres."

"The fentanyl had to have come from the Rehab Center," Pomoroy insisted. "I believe Celia Beale and/or

Pearle Key were supplying Zayres. Once he got his hands on it, he concocted his own brand of illegal drugs."

"Three times the same drug cocktail that killed Hank Night coursed through Pearle Key," said Curt. "Additionally, she was murdered on the very same day as Jersey Zayres. No doubt exists in my mind about that."

Penny scoffed. "Two murders the same day? In Chatham? Just a coincidence?" She rolled her eyes. "Nah, I don't think so."

"Exactly, my dear wife," said Curt, turning toward her. "Coincidence in this case is highly unlikely."

"Didn't Celia claim that Pearle killed Jersey out of jealousy?" asked Penny.

Pomoroy glanced at Curt. "They did have a fight over him."

"I see where you two are going with this: either Jersey Zayres or Celia Beale killed Pearle Key," said Curt, crossing his arms. "Did Celia Beale do it? Perhaps, but her size limited her to a surprise attack. The crushed hyoid bones suggest the strangulation was quick, powerfully done, making Jersey Zayres the more likely assassin."

"Celia Beale's size also limited her in murdering Jersey Zayres," said Pomoroy. He swung around and perched on the railing. "Zayres was bonked on the head. Celia Beale could have done that."

"Indubitably," said Curt.

"Was there any evidence on the push broom?" asked Penny.

"None," said Pomoroy. "I've had that checked and rechecked. As for her being anywhere near the dumpster, there was no sign of her. Cameras were out of commission. Topping it off, the rest of the evidence that may have existed on the loading dock got washed away in the downpour before the cover was set in place."

"Efforts to preserve the scene of the crime were all for naught," said Curt, peering down at his forearms peppered with freckles and carrot-colored hair. He flexed the brachioradialis muscle of his right arm. "Sadly, logic leads back to Hank doing in Jersey Zayres."

Pomoroy scratched the back of his neck. "I don't know...Zayres may have been small potatoes, but he wasn't stupid enough to whack someone out of jealousy. Just to clean up a relationship with Celia Beale? That woman is no prize. Uh-huh. Jealousy had nothing to do with it. Zayres was using Celia Beale—and/or Pearle Key—to get to the fentanyl, plain and simple."

"Maybe Pearle was going to rat on Jersey—and Celia?" asked Penny.

"There's that, too," said Pomoroy. "My gut feeling is something else hit the fan and it put the killer over the top."

"So where was Pearle murdered?" asked Penny, exasperated.

"Nowhere near that dumpster," said Curt. "It frustrates me that not even the slightest epithelial trace belonging to Pearle Key—or Celia Beale—was uncovered at that site."

Pomoroy heaved a sigh. "Zayres could have murdered Key, dumped her in the ocean then went to the Conference Center right after."

"Yeah, but did he have a boat?" asked Penny.

"None was mentioned in the property listing," said Pomoroy. "I have to dig a little deeper into that."

Penny threw her right hand into the air. "Let's put it away for the night. It's going to drive us all nuts if we don't." She took a deep breath. "Look, Curt, I know how busy you've been between the coroner's office and our practice." She wrung her hands. "Sorry I haven't been there for you."

"As chaotic as things are at times," said Curt, crossing the veranda and taking hold of her hand. "I would not have it any other way." He kissed the back of her hand. "You need time to get back on your feet after having that little buster." He noticed the way she shifted in her chair and her shallow, rapid breathing. "I must say, you do look a bit edgy."

"Edgy is not the word for it. I'm about to bust out like Mount Saint Helens!"

Curt and Pomoroy exchanged frowns. Then Curt frowned at Penny. "Well, I say then, out with it."

"I made the most incredible discovery today. I was tracing your mother's side of the family tree, and...well, did your mother ever tell you that she was born during her mother's second marriage?"

Curt felt like a right hook got him on the chin. "Grandmommy Kathleen? She was married twice?"

"If you had opened those boxes that belonged to your mother, you would have found Kathleen's journals."

"Her first husband died. Guess what his name was."

"I haven't the foggiest."

"Armand LaRosa!"

"LaRosa? As in our friends, Adam and Janice LaRosa? Emma LaRosa?"

"You got it. So I called Adam and Janice, and they went ab-so-lute-ly nuts! They're coming down tomorrow and bringing all kinds of pictures and memorabilia. Oh, Curt! Just think about all the stories they're going to tell us!"

SEPTEMBER 17 – 8:45 A.M.

CHATHAM MARINA

"Everything is going exactly as planned," Celia Beale chirped while dusting a black hair off the left shoulder of her red seersucker outfit.

Looks like Ma's finally gotten over Jersey, Quincy thought. *Not once this morning did she mention getting back all of his stuff.* He inhaled the dewy air tainted by the ebbing tide and the cheap perfume Jersey Zayres had given Celia Beale. *When is Ma going to run out of that stink juice anyway?* He squinted into the sun that was dissolving the low-lying mist draping the bent, arthritic arm known as Cape Cod. Summer dawns that brightened at a snail's pace at 4:00 A.M. were gone now and autumn crispness had replaced the August humidity.

"The day is warming up nicely, isn't it, honey?"

"Gonna be a perfect day, Ma."

"I like your outfit," she said.

He glanced down at the clothes he was wearing: red polo shirt, black Dockers, black boat shoes. "You should, Ma. You bought all this."

"I do have great taste, don't I?"

He chuckled. "I don't look half-bad, if I do say so myself," he said, but stopped short of adding: *By the time this day is over, Beverly won't think twice about Bobby! Not after that fight they had, that's for sure. Ma says Beverly really told off that pretender. He can't even call—Ma took care of that—she banned us all from taking our cell phones on this trip. So there's just no way for Bobby to spoil this day.*

"Help Beverly into the boat, honey," said Celia.

Quincy snapped back to life and zeroed in on Beverly walking down to the twenty-eight-foot high-speed boat, which had been a gift to Celia Beale from Jersey Zayres when he first took over drug trafficking in the Chatham area. Zayres used the boat only once or twice a month and when he did, he let Celia know his intentions well in advance. The boat was the only thing the local cops and the Feds didn't get their hands on, because Jersey Zayres had put it in Celia Beale's name long before the law got wise to his activities.

"I'm on it, Ma!" Quincy yelped while jumping down onto the deck. He offered his hand to Beverly. Her grief over Pearle Key was very apparent—so was her pain over Robert Pomoroy—but her hand was so soft and warm against his that, for the first time in a long time, Quincy felt truly alive.

Beverly stepped down onto the deck then half-heartedly smoothed out her cut-off blue jeans. The sleeveless eyelet blouse she was wearing looked incredibly white against her tanned skin. She had wrapped a blue windbreaker around her waist and knotted it in front.

"Here, honey."

Quincy looked up at the picnic basket in Celia's outstretched hand. "Got it, Ma."

Turning to give the basket to Beverly, he noticed, out of the corner of his eye, Celia patting her black leather belly pack. *What's she doing that for? Does she have a bellyache or something? She doesn't look sick at all. I wonder why she keeps looking around. It's almost as if...* He detected a fleeting smirk. *Wait a minute... Ma didn't invite Bobby, did she?*

Celia winked at him. "Fishermen have already left on their morning runs," she said. "It will be another hour or so before those lazy fall tourists haul their overindulged butts out for a quick sail before lunch."

"Let me take that," said Beverly.

Quincy peered down at the hand clamped to the handle of the basket. Then he peered into sapphire eyes—and he forgot all about Celia.

Beverly gave him a weak smile.

Intoxicated with the sight of Beverly, Quincy let go of the basket. His eyes followed every move she made while stowing the basket against the portside of the boat. *Can't believe she's finally back*, he thought. *What a miracle! I was sure that Ma was never going to let me talk to Beverly again—let alone the three of us boating off to Monomoy Island like this. If today works out the way I want it to, Ma and I should reconsider moving away.* He turned to Celia and whispered, "You and I got the house cleaned up real fast, Ma. Can't believe you listed it with a realtor already, but maybe we should reconsider..."

Celia cut him off, "I'm a fast worker when things need to get done. That's a fact." She shoved the beach umbrella at Quincy. "Here, take this."

Clasping the umbrella against his chest, Quincy leaned in close to Celia. "When are we going to tell Beverly?"

Celia scanned the area, patting her belly pack. "I have that all worked out, honey. Trust me."

Worried that Pomoroy might show up, Quincy asked, "Is anybody else coming, Ma?"

Instantly, her eyes narrowed, scouring the landscape. "No, why?" Her fists clenched as her teeth gnashed the way they always did when something aggravated her. Then her dark eyes zeroed in on Quincy.

He recoiled as if Celia had just smacked him, which during his growing years did happen—not as much after that. "Y-you keep looking around." Whining laced his stammers. "Tha-that's all, Ma."

Her fists unclenched. Her cool demeanor was back.

Relieved, Quincy, told himself, *Get a grip, man. Beverly is here and Bobby isn't. That's all that matters. And what fun the three of us are going to have—just like we did before Jersey Zayres came along. Wish Aunt Pearle was here. Sure is rotten what happened to her.* He shivered at the image then shook it off. *Well, I'm sure Aunt Pearle would want us to have a good time. I just know she would—even though she hated boats and water.* "All the way out to Monomoy Island for just a silly picnic," *she used to say and then goose bumps popped up all over her.* "Oh, my! All that water all around us! I just cannot tolerate this!" *Then Ma got all pissed off and...*

Quincy felt a nudge on the shoulder.

"Are you going to take this chair or what?" Celia demanded, arms extended, hands gripping a sand chair.

He snagged the sand chair and leaned it against his leg.

"Have you narrowed down where you might like to live?" Celia whispered while handing Quincy another sand chair.

"Well, I..." He looked up at her. The look of pure innocence plastered her face. "I guess...your suggestion about Italy..."

"Italy is fine with me," cut in Celia.

Quincy took the last sand chair from Celia then gathered up all three chairs. "Then again, Ma... I just don't think..."

"Perhaps, you are right, honey. Living in a foreign country these days, being American and all..."

144

"What are you two whispering about?" asked Beverly, taking the sand chairs from Quincy.

Quincy stopped dead. *How can I possibly leave Beverly? Now, that I got her back again? But how can I stay? Go against Ma?* He swallowed hard.

Beverly frowned at him then turned away to stow the chairs behind the bench seat at the stern of the boat.

"Give me a hand, honey."

Quincy blinked.

"For crying out loud!" Celia snapped. "He's off in la-la land again! Beverly, will you please come over here and help me into the boat?"

"Uhm...no, Ma," Quincy sputtered, grabbing her hand. "I gotcha. I gotcha."

Repressing aggravation, Celia stepped into the boat. "I think maybe California is a better choice to live," she said. "Don't you agree, Beverly?"

Quincy almost had a heart attack. "Ma! You let the cat out of the bag! I thought you didn't want to say anything for a while!"

"I changed my mind, honey." She chuckled and then while heading to the helm, she broke out laughing.

"What's so funny, Ma?"

"Oh, nothing...honey."

"I never thought about living anywhere other than here on the Cape," said Beverly, sagging onto the edge of the stern bench seat. She appeared to be in shock, staring at her closed fist as though she were holding something precious. Her eyes suddenly widened and she gawked at Quincy. "You're not thinking of moving away, are you?"

He skipped out of the boat, avoiding the question. He untied the stern line from the dock then said, "We thought San Diego might be a good place for me to finish my degree in marine exploration." He slid a look at Beverly and then at Celia who was putting the key into the ignition.

"The San Diego area is so wonderful," Celia crowed as the inboard motor rumbled to life. Sludge gurgled to the surface. "Lots of ocean. Weather is nice, all year long." She glanced over her shoulder and grinned at Quincy and then at Beverly.

He got the heebie-jeebies. "Sometimes, Ma, you get so weird," he mumbled, trying to pull himself together.

A wry smile ripened as Celia hooked her chin. "I don't mind leaving Cape Cod winter's behind one little bit," she said.

Quincy untied the bowline then hopped into the boat. "Full speed ahead, Ma."

"Not a good idea, honey." Her voice was sticky sweet as Celia looked over the bow and eased the throttle forward. "This is a no wake zone. I am going to be extremely careful not to leave the slightest ripple."

Coiling the stern line on the back deck, Quincy noticed Beverly gazing at her clutched fist. *She's thinking about Bobby—again,* he thought. *I just know she is.* He sucked in a huge cleansing breath then stepped over beside her. He made a feeble attempt to divert her thoughts. "Ma says the weather's nice all year long in San Diego. Better than here."

Beverly made no comment.

"Not going to be many more days like this," he said.

Moments of silence passed.

"Kind of nice the three of us having one last picnic on Monomoy before Ma and I leave," he said.

At length she said, "Yeah."

Determined to lighten her mood, Quincy rambled on, "Wow, what fun we're going to have! Just like a long time ago! Remember when we rowed those whalers that Ma and Aunt Pearle begged off fishermen, all the way out to Monomoy Island? Took us half the day to get there. Remember, Beverly? The scads of seals that surrounded the

146

whaler? Their heads bobbing in the diamond-studded sea? You and I squealed so much at those seals that our throats got raw! So bad that we could hardly talk at all the next day! Those seals looked just like buoys. 'The buoys are watching us!' we used to say. Remember, Beverly? And then we laughed like crazy and..."

"Oh, Quincy," Celia called, her tone sticky sweet. "Will you please come over here and drive the boat?"

Beverly tisked.

Quincy eyed Beverly and after a moment, said, "What?"

One side of her face drew up as Beverly looked at Quincy in a disapproving way.

"I'm waiting, honey."

Quincy hung back.

"Honey?"

Beverly's brows fused.

At a loss, Quincy stepped to the helm.

Celia leaned in close to him. "Beverly's mooning over Pomoroy, so give it a rest, honey. Everything's going to work out just fine. Trust me."

Quincy squinted over his shoulder. Beverly was rubbing her left hand up and down her arm while she gawked at her clenched right fist. "She might be thinking about Aunt Pearle, too," he whispered.

Celia straightened. "Whatever. Doesn't matter one way or the other."

"Doesn't matter, Ma?"

Celia merely grinned at the ocean ahead of the boat. "Now, honey, I don't want you to worry about a thing. Grieving and mooning days are just about over and done with."

"Ma, what are you getting at?"

The way Celia laughed sent chills up and down his spine. Then she glanced over her shoulder and called, "Come up here, sweetie."

For some strange reason, Quincy wished that Beverly would stay put, but she didn't. Tottering toward the helm, she ran into Celia.

"Make sure my baby boy stays on course and keeps it slow," Celia said, patting Beverly on the arm. "We don't need the Harbor Master hassling us, now do we, sweetie? I am going to sit back and soak up some ocean sunshine."

Beverly didn't look too pleased at all as she stepped up beside Quincy. In fact, she appeared kind of agitated, on the angry side, a lot different from the grief and heartache that weighed her down at the dock.

Quincy glanced at Celia who was sitting down on the stern seat. A look of satisfaction slathered her face. Turning sideways on the seat, she pulled her legs up onto the white cushion. She arranged her arms on top of her belly pack and then closed her eyes.

Facing forward, Quincy sucked in a chest full breath of sea air, telling himself, *Get a grip, man. There's nothing to worry about. I have Beverly by my side... at last! And that's all that matters. How can anything possibly go wrong?*

SEPTEMBER 17 – 9:00 A.M.

REHAB CENTER

"Sunday is supposed to be a day of rest, Pomoroy," Clement sniped while exiting his unmarked police car. His left hand gripped a faded Celtics travel mug just about empty of home brewed coffee. "Why aren't you in church?"

"Same reason you're not, Rodney," muttered the young Fed who was leaning against the hood of his copper Dodge Viper, his arms and ankles crossed.

Clement snorted then took a slug of coffee. He scanned the parking lot of the Rehab Center. "Mostly staff vehicles. Too early for visitors. Too late for vagrants."

The detective was still kicking himself about Hank Night. *Why was I so positive that Night killed Zayres?* he thought. *Because Pearle Key hadn't surfaced yet? Surfaced...talk about ironic... The woman surfaced on Highland Beach like a shipwrecked sailor. Only by all accounts the woman detested boats and water. But the pressure was on me. Chathamites demanded answers. A killer in their midst had them shaking in their boots. To get them off my back, I had to pin Zayres' murder on someone. Now, I've got two murders on my hands, both ongoing. Frosts my pumpkin, having to make a 180 degree turn in the Night case—in full view of everyone—including the blasted media, which of course includes that ace reporter Debra Lawless— not to mention Doc Shirlington and Pomoroy. All part of this gumshoe business, still...*

Clement sucked in the autumn morning. "Admit to being wrong in the face of better evidence," he told himself. He squinted at the young Fed. "You look like crap, Pomoroy. Forget to shower and shave this morning?"

The Fed grunted. He uncrossed his arms and ankles then stepped to the driver-side door of the Viper and opened it. The large Styrofoam cup he took out had the burgundy and light gray logo of Chatham Coffee Company emblazing the sides. He shut the door then slugged down the liquid. Focusing off into the distance, toward the Key and Beale cottages, he grunted again. Then his hand crushed the Styrofoam cup.

"What's eating at you, Pomoroy?"

Lost in deep thought, the Fed heaved an all-consuming breath then shuffled off toward the main entrance of the Rehab Center.

Clement swilled down the rest of his coffee then twisted the cover closed. "Don't answer, see if I care." He opened the driver-side door of his unmarked car and tossed the empty mug on the floor in front of the passenger seat. "Another wild goose chase." He closed the door. "This case will never end." He matched the young Fed's all-consuming breath then traipsed after him.

Pomoroy tossed the mutilated cup into the trashcan beside the main entrance as the door slid open. He disappeared inside.

The door was in the middle of closing by the time Clement got there. The motion sensor detected him then reopened. As he stepped into the building, the odor inherent of medical facilities chafed his nostrils. "Makes my belly turn up almost as much as Celia Beale's cheap perfume." His knuckles mauled his nose as the stink throttled him.

The detective caught up to the young Fed at the end of the hall where large block letters on the sign jutting out above a door proclaimed *Administration*. The door was open. Pomoroy walked right in. So did Clement.

"I had a feeling I'd see you two today," said Luella Martin, barely looking up from her desk on the right side of the door. Her slim ebony fingers rat-a-tat-tatted on her computer keyboard.

"You see us every day," griped Clement, watching Pomoroy hunker down at the desk in front of the bay window. Beyond, the September sun had risen above the rusting trees—*about a foot,* in the detective's estimation. He pictured bayberry, plum, and scrub oak turning crimson and bronze, nearly deserted beaches, and surf fishermen wearing waders and mufflers—armor against the outer beach wind and roiling tide—casting for bass. *Humph. Wouldn't mind me doing that right about now,* he thought. *Humph. The eye of day opens later and later and closes earlier and earlier—kind of like the banks down on Main Street. Can't believe winter's right around the corner...terrific... Humph. Oh, well, at least the tourist and summer people have flown the coop. Less humanity to manage. Although residents are spilling out of their cottages like sand crabs after the tide goes out. So much for less humanity... Except, one or more of them thinks he—or she— is getting away with murder—two murders! Pomoroy's convinced that Celia Beale is mixed up in all of it. So does Doc. Never know. Putting a face to these cases won't happen unless a break comes in this case. One way or the other, Doc is still P.O.ed at me for coming down so hard on Hank Night. I just needed Night to be the one who iced Zayres!*

"Yesterday afternoon's report is on top of the rest," said Luella Martin. "I'm working on last night's. You'll have it in a couple of minutes."

Clement snagged the chair to the left side the door and turned it backward. He straddled the seat then propped his elbows on the back of the chair, bracing his jawbones on his closed fists.

Time dragged as the young Fed attacked stacks of paperwork, which had accumulated since the investigation at the Rehab began months ago. As the eraser end of a pencil flipped through yesterday's report, now and then, Pomoroy stopped to scrutinize a sheet. He scratched his head with the pencil before continuing. It was obvious that he, too, was desperate for a break in the case.

"This is getting real old, Pomoroy," Clement stewed. He stretched a crick out of his back. He drummed his thick fingers on the back of the chair. "Look, Pomoroy, I got this horrendous cavernous racket way deep in my gut and it's not letting me forget that the donut and coffee I had on the way here is long gone. Time to call it a day."

"Since Pearle Key came up missing—murdered," mumbled Pomoroy as if talking to himself, "it's been harder for Celia Beale to get her hands on fentanyl."

"So much for my empty gut," muttered Clement, rolling his eyes up at the ceiling. He scratched his chin. "By now, that two-spined dogfish has got to be hitting some snags in the finance end of things."

Pomoroy clasped his head between his hands and stared at the paperwork. "And with Curt refusing to release Zayres' body for burial and turn his diamonds over to her, Celia Beale can't get any relief." The butts of his palms rubbed his temples. "So who did Hank Night? Who did Pearle Key?"

Seeing the pain that riddled Pomoroy's face, Clement put it together. "So that's what's wrong with you, Pomoroy—the girl's found out that your investigation here has to do with her old lady and now she's P.O.ed at you because you didn't tell her about it at the outset. The girl's turned you out, 'ey, Pomoroy?"

The young Fed slapped his hand on the stack of reports, startling Clement, to say nothing about how it made Luella Martin jump. "I'm telling you, Rodney! Celia Beale has got to make her move soon! Real soon!"

Clement had the same feeling. "Don't know what that move is going to be either," he said. "All right, so we think Celia Beale killed Jersey Zayres and or Pearle Key..."

Luella Martin winced.

Clement glanced at the African-American woman. "What you hear is speculation, Ms. Martin. Not one word of it is public knowledge."

She nodded.

Clement nodded back. For the first time today, he really looked at her. Her short dark hair was smooth and glossy, the bangs reaching the frames of her purple glasses. *Purple,* he thought. *Same color as her pantsuit. She looks great—except for those white clinic shoes. Must have bunions. But she'd never be seen outside this office without matching shoes.* He scanned the floor around her desk. *Where's her purple shoes?* He squinted at the bookcase to her right. *Bingo! Purple heels!* His eyes climbed the shelves to the middle one. *And there's her purple pocketbook!* Swollen with pride, he glanced at Pomoroy. His mood fizzled.

"Celia Beale's the kind of vermin that doesn't like getting her hands dirty," said the downcast Pomoroy.

Clement twisted up the side of his face. "Carbon copy of Zayres." He scratched the back of his head. "So the dogfish doesn't have a fence. She needs cash. What is her next move going be?"

"Here's last night's report," said Martin, plopping paperwork on the desk beside Pomoroy.

Pomoroy gave the report an acknowledging glimpse then continued to dissect the older reports. His eyes suddenly narrowed, as if somebody aimed a spotlight at him.

Clement perked up. "Got something?"

Pomoroy gawked at the latest report. "Celia Beale pulled a double shift last night."

Clement rolled his eyes. "So?"

Pomoroy leaned over the new report and at length, mumbled, "Hmm...Three patients croaked last night..." He picked up the report and straightened. "While under her care." His eyes dissected the first page. He flipped to the second page. His eyes dissected that page. "Pharmacy report shows all three patients were prescribed three days of fentanyl patches." He looked up. "Didn't I tell you, Rodney?"

"Tell me what?"

"Celia Beale got her hands on fentanyl last night. She's about to cut and run."

"And you know that how?"

"Things have been strange."

"Strange? Is that all you got, Pomoroy?" Clement got no answer. "You and the girl have a spat—that's what is making things strange to you." Clement shook his head. "Look, Pomoroy, it just doesn't add up. So the dogfish needs money. We both know there's no new fence and..."

"Celia Beale is doing her own fencing," cut in Pomoroy.

"You got proof?"

Pomoroy jabbed his finger on a particular line item and turned to Luella Martin. "What about this drug? Pan...cu...something-or-other. It hasn't shown up before in any other report."

Luella Martin stepped over to the young Fed and took a look at where his finger was pointing. Confusion sheeted her face. "Pancuronium bromide."

"What's it do?" pressed Pomoroy.

She took off her glasses and gestured with them. "It's a neuro-muscular blocking agent—a skeletal muscle relaxant used during surgery to keep patients' muscles from moving while keeping them awake. We use it here to treat ARDS."

Pomoroy gave her a blank stare.

She blinked. "Adult Respiratory Distress Syndrome."

The young Fed let that sink in for a moment. "Muscle relaxant."

"A paralytic," added Martin, putting on her glasses. She studied the pharmacy report. "Wow, there's quite a lot of doses listed here."

"More than three?" asked Clement.

"Three times three—at least," said Martin.

A melody escaped Pomoroy and then lyrics to a song, "*One pill makes you larger...*"

Clement scratched his chin. "If memory serves me right, that's the drug used on death row prisoners just before the ultimate lethal injection."

"I got a feeling that those three patients didn't die of their illness," said Martin. "I am going to immediately initiate a full scale investigation of every single drug that has ever come through the doors of this institution— where, what, when, how, and how much was actually used."

"I'll bet autopsies on the three patients who croaked last night will detect the presence of pancuronium bromide," said Clement.

Martin nodded. "Its marker is identifiable in cadavers for months...that is, if an autopsy is ever performed. In cases like these, next of kin rarely ask for autopsies because they feel it desecrates the body of their loved one whom they feel has been through quite enough."

Clement felt the muscle on the side of his neck contract. "Celia Beale lifted enough of that juice to take down an elephant."

"How about a herd of elephants?" sniped Martin.

Pomoroy droned on, *"And the one that Mother gives you…"*

"Pomoroy! Why in God's name are you chanting *Go Ask Alice?*'" demanded Clement. Of course, he received no response.

"Celia Beale is not allowed access to pancuronium bromide," commented Martin.

"Certainly looks like the ornery dogfish has got her hands on it," Clement growled while reaching into his pocket for his vibrating cell phone. "Plenty of it!" He squinted at the caller ID then flipped open the lid. "Mornin', Doc!"

"Shoot," belched Pomoroy, gawking at his watch. "I was supposed to be at Curt's an hour ago!" He leapt to his feet. "Tell him I'm on my way!"

Waving off the young Fed, Clement spoke into the phone. "Say, Doc, what do you suppose Celia Beale is going to do with mega doses of a paralytic drug?" The information that came back to him assaulted his senses, beating him worse than a gale upon an unreefed mainsail. He could feel those nasty red splotches chafing his body. "Why that insatiable dogfish!" He sprang to his feet.

"What's up, Rodney?" asked Pomoroy.

Again, Clement waved off the young Fed. "We're on our way, Doc! Yeah, yeah, I'll fill Pomoroy in!"

"Rodney? What's going on?"

Clement flipped the lid of the cell phone closed as he hauled butt out of the room.

"Stop, Rodney!"

Seconds later, Clement sensed the young Fed breathing down his neck.

"Rodney! I said stop! Tell me what's going on right now! Rodney!"

This time, it was Clement who didn't answer.

SEPTEMEMBER 17 – 10:00 A.M.

SHIRLINGTON RESIDENCE

Curt stuck out his hand as Adam LaRosa stepped onto the veranda. Instead of a handshake, he found himself trapped in a bear hug.

"Hey, there, cousin!" Adam exclaimed.

"Well!" Curt blustered. "I must say!"

Adam held Curt at arms' length. "Welcome to the LaRosa family!" He released Curt then lightly punched him on the arm. "Looks like you and Penny aren't at the end of your family trees after all!"

"The news certainly bowled me over," Curt said. Regaining his footing, he scanned the neighborhood. As luck would have it, not a soul had seen the spectacle...well, only a squirrel, its supple body drawing happy arcs beneath the hundred-year oak. Curt did not consider himself a prude, although he did feel somewhat relieved as he smoothed out his clothes.

"Where is our little Jeffrey?" Janice squealed as she wobbled up the stairs of the veranda. In her arms was an enormous box of LaRosa family pictures and memorabilia.

"Here, let me take that," Curt said, latching onto the box.

Penny's voice rang out from inside the cottage. "Here comes J. C.!"

Curt raced to the screen door and managed to get it open just as Penny, babe in arms, reached it.

"Oh-h, let me have my precious little cousin," Janice cooed, her hands extending, her fingers wriggling.

Braced against the open screen door, Curt smiled at the scene. Penny was flushing all over. As she shifted Jeffrey into Janice's arms, jasmine and honeysuckle perfumes fused with the aroma of baby shampoo.

"Oh-h, look at you," Janice clucked, in awe of the baby. "So alert and bright... So sweet... Absolutely perfect! You look so much like my little Augie..." Tears welled in her eyes. She massaged her cheek against the fuzzy little pate. "M-m-m... There is nothing like the smell of a baby."

Curt coughed away the sadness that tinged the air. "Do come in, folks," he said.

During brunch, Adam said, "You are aware, Curt, that your father and mother met in the Berkshires, correct?"

"Indeed," Curt said, in the midst of finishing off his second cup of tea. "Father was an upstart instructor at Williams College, having arrived from London several months prior to meeting Mother. During their courtship, Boston University offered a position to Father, which precipitated the marriage to Mother and their subsequent relocation to Boston."

Adam put down his coffee then got up from the table to get the box of pictures and memorabilia that was setting on the bar. "According to my mother..."

"The late, great Emma LaRosa," cut in Janice, gesturing with the partially eaten English muffin topped with raspberry jam. "The last great storyteller of the family."

Adam began again, "According to my mother, your grandmother Kathleen had two children from her first marriage to my Uncle Armand," Adam said, placing the box on the table. "He was all mixed up in the mafia, but wanted out. Nobody except my Uncle Rom, who was a cop, knew that Uncle Armand was working both ends from the middle."

"It was inevitable that the mafia found out," Janice said.

"And of course, they whacked him," Penny said, while burping Jeffrey.

Adam swallowed hard, nodding. "A message to others that ratting results in grave consequences."

"You know how it was back then," cut in Janice. "Italians and Irish did not mix, so nobody even conceived of Armand and Kathleen having anything to do with each other, let alone being married."

"Again, the only one who knew Kathleen existed at all was my Uncle Rom," Adam said. "Come to find out, after Uncle Armand was killed, his two kids came to light."

"Aldo and Angelatina," Janice added. "Kathleen was scared to death for them."

"Rightfully so," Curt said, resting his arms on the table.

Janice took the lid off the box then leaned close to Penny. "Armand left Kathleen quite a stash, you know."

"Bet the mafia wanted to get its hands on that," Penny said.

"You bet," Adam said. "So Kathleen took off for the Berkshires."

"Back then, that was a huge distance from Boston," Janice said.

"She stopped in Springfield," Adam went on, "and picked up documents that changed her last name."

"Which of course, must have included Aldo and Angelatina's last name," said Janice.

"According to my mother," Adam said, "Uncle Armand laid out the plan, years before the mafia got him, and stashed away every document Kathleen might ever need..."

"Along with loads of money," added Janice.

"...In a safety deposit box in Springfield," continued Adam. "Just before dying from gunshot wounds, Uncle Armand gave Uncle Rom the key to another safety deposit box located in Boston. There was a sealed envelope for Kathleen and also one for my grandmother, Maria Avita."

"Later on," Janice said, "we'll tell you about Father Sandro's money and how it figured into the mix." Her eyebrows jiggled. "That's a story in itself!"

Adam held up an ordinary piece of lined stationary, yellow from age. "This is the letter Uncle Armand left for my grandmother."

Curt drew in a breath then took the letter. He found it difficult reading Armand's scrawl:

Dear Mamacita,

This is the hand of cards the Man Upstairs dealt for me. Life just played out the game. For years, I have loved Kathleen with all my heart and soul, but I thought that how mixing Irish blood with LaRosa blood would cause great anguish. On the other hand, I think you should know - no, I *want* you to know! You have two grandchildren by me—a boy, Aldo, and a girl, Angelatina.

"According to my mother," Adam said, "Grandpa Joseph called my grandmother Angelatina *mia*. Uncle Armand goes on to say that Kathleen had no family and he did not want her and the children alone in this world. He was afraid that she might one day be a vendetta target."

Curt studied the handwriting then handed the letter back to Adam. He built a pyramid with his arms and tapped his fingers on his chin. "So what you are telling me is my mother was not of Scottish origin, but of Irish."

"I assume that was part of Uncle Armand's plan," Adam said.

"Logic being Kathleen could not hide her red hair and blue eyes," Curt said.

"She may have used a dark henna to cover up her hair color," Janice suggested. "Lots of women used henna back then."

"Henna," mused Curt. "Taking a step away from being Irish to being Scottish afforded her and the two children a certain degree of protection."

"Henna," Penny said.

"Camouflage," Curt said.

Janice sent Curt and Penny a confused leer then handed Curt a grainy yellow photograph, "Here's a picture of Kathleen."

Curt studied the image. "Uncanny resemblance to my own dear Mum."

"Weird, huh?" commented Adam. "That picture and the story that surrounds it has been staring us right in the eyes for decades." He reached into the box. "This is a picture of my grandparents, Maria Avita and Joseph and their eight children. It was taken shortly before my Aunt Francesca died in the Molasses Flood of 1919." He pointed at faces, so familiar to generations of LaRosas. "This is Uncle Armand. And this is my Uncle Rom—that's a World War I uniform he's wearing. He left for war the same day this picture was taken. Everybody says I look like him."

"Indubitably," Curt said. "I would have been privileged to knowing the LaRosa clan."

Penny held Jeffrey close as she leaned over and squinted at the picture. "Uncle Rom sure looks so familiar."

"No way you knew him," Adam said.

Penny straightened, deep in thought.

"You've known me quite a while," Adam said, "but Curt's known me a lot longer—even before I got this gray."

161

"White, honey," Janice taunted while picking at his hair. "White."

Penny didn't react to the humor. Instead, her head cocked to one side as she scrutinized Adam. "No, not *your* face..." She squinted at the picture again. "Why can't I place that face?"

A moment of silence passed. Bewildered, Adam cleared his throat. "Well, let's see..." He sifted through more pictures.

"Wait!" Penny cried, clamping her hand on Adam's wrist.

Brows came together as everyone gawked at her.

Penny grabbed a picture and waved it at Adam and Janice. "Who is this?"

"Why, that's our Autumn," Janice yelped.

Penny and Curt exploded in unison, "Your daughter!"

"Y-Yes," Janice stammered. "Autumn is a junior in high school. I know you haven't seen her in a very long time. And I'm so sorry that she and Eliot didn't come today. But you know how teenagers are. Hanging out with parents is not cool. Not only that, they both work after school—and on weekends. They send their love, of course."

Curt stared at Penny whose face had drained of color. Her toffee-colored eyes were big as ping pong balls. He sensed he displayed a similar deportment.

Adam spoke up, "Stop worrying, you two. Big brother Eliot is keeping an eye on Autumn."

"Eliot is worse than we are in that respect," Janice said, taking Adam's hand. They exchanged uneasy glances.

"Clearly, you misread our agitation," Curt said.

"Agitation?" Adam asked, frowning. "Hey, what the heck is the matter with you two?"

Curt got to his feet and paced. "Salt water removed the henna from Pearle Key's hair," he mumbled—as if he

162

was the only person in the room. "Strands of natural color belonging to Pearle Key did not match Beverly's. Curious. English women of her age—and that of Celia Beale—rarely experience qualms to the natural aging process. Celia Beale has a slight English accent. Again curious. The rage these days is to flaunt one's accent—unless..." He stopped pacing and gaped at Penny.

"Unless they are hiding something," Penny said.

"My dear Penny, are you thinking along the same lines as I?"

She nodded. "Quincy and Beverly."

"Beverly?" Janice asked.

"The girl whose mother was murdered," Janice said.

"The very same lass Robert is dating," Curt said.

Penny recoiled. "Oh, shoot! Robert and Beverly had a fight, yesterday. I promised him I'd call her..."

Curt butted in, "You talked to Beverly about her hair."

Penny nodded. "A couple of times. It's gotten so long and out of shape. The color is so ratty. I told her she should go get it cut and colored—at least the ends anyways until the junk grows out. I told her I'd even do it if she wanted me to, but she keeps putting it off."

Adam looked completely lost. Janice had the deer-in-the-headlights stare.

"Beverly is not ready for any change," Curt said, pacing again.

"Yeah," Penny said. "Pearle's murder is enough change. You know, I even suggested that she go with me to my hairdresser the next time I go. I told her I love the color of her roots and she should go back to her natural color."

"Auburn," added Curt. He stopped. He was facing the wall, but the flowery wallpaper didn't register in his mind. "Auburn roots..."

Penny gasped. "Just like Autumn's."

Curt turned and faced Penny, gawking back and forth at the picture in her hands and then at Janice.

Janice wrung her hands, making an effort to smile, but her lips merely wrinkled. "I-I don't understand..."

"These days, Quincy is sporting a flattop," Curt said.

"Beverly heard that he actually went to Wes' Barbershop to get it done," Penny said. "I think he looks great, but according to Beverly, Celia would never have cut his hair like that."

"A flattop that leaves dark brown roots," mused Curt.

"And a few blond tips," Penny added. "Celia and Pearle used way too much henna. Pearle dumped henna on Beverly all her life and Celia bleached Quincy's hair...all his life. Those two kids never once saw the inside of a hair salon."

Curt rubbed his chin between his thumb and forefinger. "Hmm, that fight Pearle Key and Celia Beale had over Jersey Zayres... Jealousy? Curious indeed."

"Robert insists Celia was supplying Jersey with drugs from the Rehab Center," Penny said. "Pearle must've found out, and I bet she was going to the cops."

"No," Curt said. "Pearle Key knew about the drug trafficking—and I suspect she may have even participated. No, the motive had to be more than a threat of exposure or jealousy. Even the two combined."

Adam spoke up. "Interesting how you two take things apart, but..."

"Hold it!" Penny exclaimed. "Jersey found out about..." She covered her mouth and glanced at Adam and Janice.

Curt took a quick step back, thinking, *That's it! Jersey Zayres discovered the truth about Summer and August LaRosa and he was blackmailing Celia Beale and Pearle Key into obtaining drugs from the Rehab Center. One or both of the women threatened to give it all up to law enforcement. That certainly would have put Celia Beale over the top. Perhaps she was bent on stopping Pearle Key from giving up the twins—especially, Quincy. Perhaps Celia Beale urged Jersey Zayres to stop Pearle Key and in the process he decided both women were detrimental to his illegal livelihood. A woman of Celia Beale's volatility surely made the drug business much too precarious. Now, that makes sense. Aye, Jersey Zayres killed Pearle Key while Celia Beale was at work, which was her alibi. He met with Celia Beale later, intent on murdering her. But on the loading dock behind the Conference Center? And how did Celia Beale end up killing him?*

"Celia had to be the one who killed Jersey," Penny said.

"But why didn't we find evidence?" Curt asked. "Not one of her fingerprints was found. Then that poor ol' sod Hank Night came along and spotted Jersey Zayres run through with a metal corner protector."

"Jersey's ring and ear studs must've really tempted Hank," Curt said.

Adam jounced his hands. "Can Janice and I participate in this conversation?"

"Hank climbed down into that dumpster," Penny suggested, "and took all of Jersey's valuables—including the drug that killed him."

Adam rolled his eyes and tisked.

Penny gasped. "Those drugs were meant for Celia! But she got the drop on him!"

"If that's the scenario," Curt said, "why did Hank confess on his deathbed?"

"Maybe he believed he did kill Jersey," Penny suggested.

"Believed his own lie?" Curt asked.

Penny nodded. "Why not? Rodney kept repeating the lie—over and over and over again."

"Badgering," Curt said. "So much that a lie became the truth in a terminal mind. With luck and a confession, the ol' sod was led into believing that by confessing, his days of being a bad liar were over and done with, forgiven, and therefore, the Heavenly Gates were going to open for him."

"You were right all along, Curt. Hank did not kill Jersey. Nope. Celia Beale did it and..." Penny gasped. "Curt! Quincy could have been Rom's twin."

Adam jumped to his feet. "Now look you two!"

Janice rushed to Adam's side and clasped her arms about his waist. Years of false hopes that her twins would be returned to her had taken its toll. She used to be a fighter. She used to believe what Emma always said, "Time has a way of working things out." Not anymore. Janice shriveled like a whipped puppy.

Curt studied the LaRosa family picture taken just before Francesca drowned in molasses. He looked up and encountered the tormented face of Adam LaRosa whose wife was sobbing against his chest. His mind burned with speculation: *Quincy Beale could be Adam's twin. Is he truly Adam's son, August? The brother of fraternal twin, Summer? AKA Beverly Key?* Curt eyeballed Penny again. She was staring at the picture of Adam and Janice's teenage daughter. *A miraculous turnaround indeed.*

"Curt, tell them," Penny whispered.

"Tell us what?" Adam demanded.

Curt ran his hand through his hair. "My dear wife, what if we are wrong? This extraordinary couple has suffered enough. They don't need us to..."

"For God's sake!" Adam exclaimed. "Please stop this nonsense immediately!"

"Curt," Penny said, taking his hand. "You know in your soul, we are not wrong."

Somehow, Curt managed to get the words out: "Penny and I believe..." His heart thumped all the way up into his throat. He swallowed it back. He took a deep breath and started again. "Penny and I believe that we have discovered the whereabouts of Summer and August."

Summer And August

SEPTEMBER 17 – 10:00 A.M.

CELIA'S HIGH-SPEED BOAT

Beverly tilted her head toward Quincy and whispered, "Hey!" She knew without looking that his focus was shifting to her. She sensed the happiness that oozed from his every pore. But this trip to Monomoy Island was all wrong. Her wary eyes signaled once over her shoulder.

"What's going on?" he asked.

She put her index finger to her lips. "Sh-sh-sh!" Her stomach churned like a caldron as her eyes guardedly ping ponged between him and Celia. The snoozing woman appeared to be lightly snoring.

Confusion tightened his demeanor. He squinted at Beverly then checked the heading of the boat making way through the Stage Harbor Channel. He glanced over his shoulder at Celia and then squinted at Beverly.

She toggled her line of sight between him and her fist shielded against her stomach. Her fingers opened out like a rose bud.

"An earring," Quincy said. He peered sideways at the forty-eight foot cast-iron Stage Harbor Lighthouse that was passing beyond the stern on the starboard side. "So what?"

Beverly closed her fist, bug-eying Quincy. "Don't talk so loud!"

His eyes riveted on her. "What is going on?" he whispered.

They both glanced over their shoulders at Celia.

Beverly held back strands of hair flogging the side of her face as wind spilled over the bow of the boat and parted the hair at the back of her head.

Celia's face twitched. Her hands seemed to be kneading her black leather belly pack.

Beverly and Quincy gawked at one another. They turned forward.

"Can't believe I didn't bring my cell phone," Beverly grumbled.

"How come?"

She shot a sidelong look at him. Out of the corner of her mouth, she whispered, "The earring belonged to Mom. It's part of the set I gave her for her last birthday."

His eyes narrowed on the earring in her hand.

She pointed to the semiprecious gem. "That's Mom's birthstone."

"You know I hate riddles, Beverly," he groused, staring over the bow as the boat headed into open water.

Beverly huffed. "Get a grip, Quincy. I found this earring in the corner of the deck when I was stowing the picnic basket. Quincy! Mom never set one foot on this boat! And this is the first time for me!"

"You get a grip, Beverly! You know I know all that!"

"So how did her earring end up on the deck, Quincy?" She bit her lip, afraid to tell him what she was really thinking.

Like so many times throughout their young lives, they read each other's thoughts.

"Somehow, Jersey got Aunt Pearle onto this boat," he said.

"Amazing," said Beverly.

"Considering how much she hated that jerk and how much she hated water and boats," said Quincy.

Beverly shivered. "Oh, Quincy... I didn't want to think... I didn't want to say..."

He tightened his grip on the steering wheel. Monomoy Island loomed ahead. Seal heads bobbed in the diamond-studded sea. "I bet that jerk killed Aunt Pearle. Yup. Then took her body out to sea. When he thought he was far enough offshore, he dumped her."

"That's how Mom ended up on Highland Beach," Beverly said.

"Her earring probably fell off as he either loaded her body onto the boat or dumped it overboard," Quincy said. "Maybe Bobby and the cops were right about Aunt Pearle all along."

Beverly groaned. "No, I don't believe for one minute that Mom was dealing drugs."

Quincy got the urge to goose the high-speed boat. Perhaps then this conversation would stop. Perhaps then all those great feelings he had about today would come flooding back. *Fat chance.* He sighed. "Ma and I knew all along that Jersey was making a stash of dough off drugs. But Ma said we shouldn't talk about it because Jersey could get real mean."

"Maybe Mom found out that Jersey was stealing drugs at the Rehab Center," said Beverly. "Maybe she tried to stop him and that's why he killed her."

Quincy winced. "Sure makes sense, doesn't it?"

Beverly managed a shrug. "What should we do, Quincy?"

"Heck if I know."

"Without our cell phones," Beverly said, "we don't have too many options."

"I say none at all," Quincy said.

"Do you suppose Aunt Celia brought hers?" Beverly ventured. "You know...just in case of an emergency?"

They glanced over their shoulders.

Beverly held back strands of hair flogging the side of her face.

Celia snorted in her sleep. Her hand shifted ever so slightly over the belly pack.

Beverly and Quincy eyed one another.

He looked out over the bow of the boat. "Geez, Beverly. I really don't want to spoil the day because of that jerk. He spoiled too many things already."

Beverly eyed Quincy as he checked out Celia again then stared straight ahead. Obviously, he was avoiding eye contact. "Quincy?"

He rolled his eyes. "Look, Beverly, today is the last chance Ma and I will ever have before..." Suddenly, he clammed up.

"Don't pretend you're keeping track on where we're going," she whispered. "You're just avoiding me—just like you're pretending to be avoiding seals in the water. You're just faking—just like Bobby's been doing all this time. Faking. Aargh! You're all the same!"

Quincy reeled. "Hey, don't compare me to Bobby! *I* would have told you about the Rehab investigation!"

"Bobby did tell me," she countered.

"He didn't tell you Aunt Pearle had anything to do with it," Quincy jabbed.

Beverly hung her head, waving it side to side. "I didn't have a clue until Aunt Celia told me. But Mom stealing drugs? Come on, Quincy." She looked up at him. "You know Mom better than that."

He nodded. "She would never steal drugs—or anything else for that matter."

"Stealing just wasn't in her at all," Beverly said. "How can Bobby even think a thing like that?"

"He didn't know Aunt Pearle like you and me."

Guilt raced through Beverly. "Oh, why didn't Bobby tell me everything? Then I wouldn't have gotten so mad at him. He's never going to forgive me."

"You think *he* should forgive *you*?"

"Well," she stammered, "yeah." She looked back toward Chatham. "Wonder where he is?"

Quincy looked back, too. "All this gives me the creeps."

She sighed. "Maybe Bobby thinks I'm not worth all the hassle and is gone for good. Gone..." She glared at Quincy. "You're really going away! Aren't you?"

His jaw tightened as he refocused ahead.

"Look at me, Quincy! You and Aunt Celia are not just talking about leaving! You are actually going to go!"

Suddenly conscious of the level of their voices, they glanced over their shoulders. Celia was snoozing undisturbed. Relief sheeted over them. Beverly narrowed her vision on Quincy. His eyes met hers then quickly shifted at the sea ahead of them.

"How can you do that to me, Quincy?" she whispered through her teeth. "How can you move away and leave me all alone when you know I don't have Mom anymore? I don't even have Bobby anymore!"

Quincy took one hand off the wheel and jounced it, palm up. "Look, Beverly, Jersey and Aunt Pearle's murders have just been too much for Ma and me, so..."

"Too much for you?" Her brows tightened. "What about me? My Mom was murdered! How would you feel if it was your *Ma* who turned up dead on that beach? You don't have a clue about what I have been going through, do you?"

By the look on his face, there was no doubt that her words stung him worse than a hive of riled up mud wasps.

She turned her back on him and crossed her arms over her chest. "Oh, I can't believe this! I really thought you cared about me!"

"You know I do, Beverly."

She looked up at the sky. "Then how come you stayed away?"

"Ma wouldn't..."

173

"Lame, Quincy, real lame." She rolled her eyes and shook her head side-to-side. She leered at the seals frolicking in the diamond-studded sea. She leered at the beach where the Keys and Beales picnicked in the past. So many carefree days. Monomoy Island was getting closer and closer and she would do anything not to go there. She didn't want to be anywhere with Quincy. She didn't want to be anywhere with Celia. All she wanted to do was to go back to Chatham. She wanted to find Bobby. She wanted to beg for his forgiveness. Was that too much to ask?

"You don't know how many times I wanted to stand up to Ma. Honest, Beverly. I really did, but..."

She spun around. "But guts are part of it!"

He hung his head and mumbled, "Yeah."

"You should've had guts enough to stand up to her, Quincy."

He gazed out over the bow of the boat. At length he sighed. "I love you, Beverly."

She shot a look at him. "What?"

His soulful eyes fell upon her. "I always have and I didn't have the guts to tell you either."

Her insides turned to mush. "Well, I always loved you, too, but..."

"Not the way I love you. I want you to love me like...like..." His eyes turned away from hers.

"Like what, Quincy?" She grabbed his forearm. "Like what?"

He shook off her hand as frustration wrinkled his face. His head bounced around like a bobble head figurine. He stiffened suddenly then his fist smacked the steering wheel.

She took a step back, gaping at him. "Oh, I get it. You want me to love you like I love Bobby. That's it, isn't it?"

"That guy's been hanging around you ever since..."

Anger bubbled to the surface. "Go ahead, Quincy, say it!" She got in his face, lashing out, "Say, 'Since Mom came up missing! Since Jersey Zayres *murdered* Mom! Since that janitor killed Jersey! Since everything's been going so completely nuts!' Get a grip Quincy! If I didn't have Bobby, I wouldn't have had anybody! And I would have been going nuts!" She fought to hold back the tears that burned her eyes like brine. "All because you don't have guts enough to stand up to *Ma*! And be there when I needed you! That's no way to love somebody, Quincy! Bobby's been my strength. He's been the one who got me through it all. He came out of nowhere and without ever being asked, he stuck by me! The way you should have, Quincy! You should have been there for me! You should have been there!"

His jaw tightened. Clearly, he was also holding back the tears as he aimed the boat between a couple groups of seals then toward the beach.

She folded her arms and turned her back to him. "Worst of all, I should've been there for Bobby. I should have had more faith in him. How could I have been so stupid?"

"I'm so sorry, Beverly. I'm going to make all of it up to you, just wait and see. Everything's going to be just like it used to be."

She spiraled back to him. "Used to be? How? By having one last happy-go-lucky picnic on Monomoy Island and then deserting me?"

"I'm not going to desert you." His voice was low and mellow. "No, I'm not going anywhere anymore. I'm staying right here in Chatham...with you."

"What about her?" Beverly hooked her thumb over her shoulder and jabbed it at Celia.

He looked back. His eyes slitted. "Ma can go if she wants to." He didn't even try to whisper.

Celia twitched in her sleep. Her fingers were burrowed into her belly pack.

His eyes softened as Quincy looked at Beverly. "I'm staying with you."

She sagged. "When are you going to tell her?"

He glanced ahead, chewing the inside of his left cheek.

"And when are you going to tell her that Jersey murdered Mom?"

He pulled back the throttle and the boat drifted into shore.

"When, Quincy?"

"Ma's devastated over Jersey's murder as it is. When she finds out he murdered Aunt Pearle... Wow, that will really put Ma over the edge. Can't we just let it go, just for a few hours?"

They braced themselves as the boat grounded on the sandy beach. The tide was halfway to its ebb, which gave them hours to spend here. By the time it came to leaving, the tide would be coming in again. All they would have to do is wait a few minutes for the boat to be afloat and then they would be off to Chatham. It wasn't soon enough for either one of them.

Choking back frustration, Quincy said, "Please, Beverly?"

She peered sideways at him. "Promise when we get back, we'll tell Bobby right away?"

He cut the engine. "You're going back to Bobby." It wasn't a question. It was a statement of fact.

Water lapped the shore. Somewhere a seagull squawked.

Beverly swallowed hard. "Promise me, Quincy."

His face twisted up. A moment passed. His entire frame relaxed as he sighed. "Yeah. I promise."

SEPTEMBER 17 – 11:00 A.M.

MONOMOY ISLAND

"Ma, Wake up," Quincy said, giving her a nudge. "We're here."

"Oh, I wasn't sleeping, honey," Celia breezed. She patted her black leather belly pack.

"Sure, Ma."

Quincy glanced anxiously at Beverly who looked like she had just bit into a sour pickle. Her left foot was kicking up a spatter of sand and shells. Her right fist was clutching the earring tight to her heart. Her left hand was rubbing her right bicep.

He looked back at Celia yawning in the midst of a catlike stretch. He got real bad vibes when she scanned the ocean and the long strand of beach and said, "Looks like we got the whole place to ourselves."

He swallowed hard. "How great is that?"

"What is that, honey?"

He winced. "Oh, I was just thinking about our cell phones back home."

Celia snickered. "Cells will not work out here anyway. Now, give me a hand."

He hesitated, squinted at her outstretched hand then at her.

She jounced her hand.

He took hold of it and managed to support her as she stepped out of the boat.

"You two have been busy," Celia said, smoothing wrinkles out of her red seersucker outfit. She flicked a speck off her shoulder then her black eyes dissected him.

He gave her a blank stare.

A smile wrinkled her lips.

Suddenly, Quincy felt sick to his stomach.

She patted him on the back with one hand and pointed with the other. "The picnic basket? The beach umbrella? Sand chairs?"

Tongue-tied, he glanced at the supplies stacked up a short distance away, basking in the sun against the dune that was a part of the spine that ran the length of Monomoy Island. He peered down at her face grinning up at him.

"You are a fast worker when things need to get done," Celia said, winking at Quincy. "That's a fact. Well, now, you must be parched. I know I am. How about you, sweetie?" Those black eyes of hers focused on Beverly who was standing in front of the boat. "Say, what's that you have in your hand?"

Suddenly, Quincy got the urge to jump in front of Beverly and shield her with his body. But he didn't and he was incensed with himself. *What is wrong with me? And why do I have to protect Beverly from Ma anyway?*

Beverly looked down at her fist and it seemed for a moment, she might open it. But then her eyes grew wide and her knuckles turned white. She gaped into the distance—toward Chatham.

He wished the day was over and done with and they were on their way home—and he didn't know why.

Celia took a step toward Beverly.

"Ma!"

Celia stopped. Her eyes narrowed on Quincy.

"Beverly is thirsty," he stammered. "She told me so...just before I woke you up. She misses Bobby... That's all, Ma. Don't worry about it."

178

"Oh, I am not worrying at all, honey," Celia said in a singsong voice. "Not today." She offered her arm to him.

He made no move to take it.

Celia entwined her right arm in his then tugged him over to Beverly "No, honey, you are not going to catch *me* worrying about one little thing on this glorious day."

It felt wrong for him to hook his elbow around Beverly's—and yet, that lifetime connection between Beverly and him made it right. *Weird,* Quincy thought. *On one side of me, I get the creeps and on the other side, I feel whole.*

Arm-in-arm, the three headed toward the picnic supplies.

"I made fresh lemonade for the both of you," Celia said.

"Yum," Quincy said.

Celia let go of Quincy then squatted next to the picnic basket. "Well, here we are, at last." She opened the lid and took out the blanket. "Here. You two spread this out."

Quincy took the blanket from her. Separating the corners of the blanket, he kept two for himself and handed the other two to Beverly. They stepped away from one another, opening up the blanket. Then they bent at the knees and spread it on the sand.

All the while, Quincy and Beverly were keeping their wary eyes on Celia. *Look at her surveying the area,* their brains seemed to tell each other. *Her hand keeps rubbing that belly pack. She keeps dissecting everything. Horizon. Sky. Dune. Water. Even that nosey seal that popped its head out of the water over there. That silly thing is trying to figure out what's going on—this beach belongs to him. What are these gatecrashers doing here?*

Celia rolled down onto the blanket and smiled with satisfaction. "Now, how about that lemonade?" She took packages of sandwiches and chips out of the picnic basket.

179

"Here you are, you little devils," she hissed and then pulled out two quart-size thermoses. The third one she took out, she held up for Quincy to see. "My special brew of iced tea." She winked at him.

Her favorite booze of the day is in that thermos, he thought. He turned away and opened the umbrella. *Sure hope Ma doesn't get pickled today. That will spoil everything—worse than telling her about the earring Beverly found and what we think Jersey did to Aunt Pearle. As much as I despised that jerk, I sure hope it's not true.* He glanced at Beverly who was arranging the sand chairs beneath the umbrella. *She looks so stressed out.*

Celia popped the plug on her thermos then took several long slugs.

Quincy jammed his hands into his hips. "Ma!"

Celia stopped, her mouth bulging with liquid.

He exchanged frowns with Beverly. He looked back at Celia. Thinking quick, he said, "Are you ever going to get around to giving us our drinks, Ma?"

Celia swallowed. "Oh, honey, I am so sorry." She smacked her lips. "I was just so thirsty and..."

He melted onto one of the sand chairs.

"You are picking on me, aren't you, honey?"

He managed a weak smile.

"You better sit down, too, sweetie," said Celia. Her open palm, face up, gestured to the sand chair next to Quincy. "We cannot afford to spill one single drop. These three thermoses are all we have to drink today."

"Why didn't you bring more?" asked Quincy, watching Beverly lower herself on the sand chair.

"It simply slipped my mind, honey," Celia breezed. She handed a thermos to Beverly. "Ladies first." Then she handed the other thermos to Quincy. She waited, watching him and Beverly pull up the plugs that doubled as straws. "Okay, now, you two know the rules! Clink your thermoses together then drink as much as you can to make sure the utmost of luck comes our way! Ready? One! Two! Three!"

Quincy and Beverly clinked thermoses then took several long pulls and came up out of breath. As his tongue twisted with a bitter aftertaste, he couldn't help but notice the way Celia seemed to be biding her time. "How come you didn't drink any of yours, Ma?"

Her charm evaporated quicker than spit on an August sidewalk. Her eyes hardened into black ice. "Are you actually that stupid to think I am just going to walk away and let you stay in Chatham? With Beverly?"

Quincy went to get up, instinct driving him to protect Beverly, but the world began to swim around him, round and round, faster and faster. His brain and vision fogged like a windshield on a muggy night. His jaw went slack. "Wh-a-..." His words slopped out of his mouth as if they were coming from a drunkard. "...goin'...on?"

His head drooped forward as his entire body slumped. His head lolled to his right and smacked into his shoulder. He tried to cry out, *Beverly!* But his mouth refused to function. His head slipped off his shoulder and plopped onto the back of the sand chair. *I feel like a ragdoll with no joints, hurtling through some sort of cosmic fracture. Lost.*

A voice from far, far away cried out, *Get a grip!*
Beverly! Where are you?

"Here, look at me, Quincy!" snapped Celia as her fingers drilled into his chin and yanked his head forward.

Quincy? She never calls me Quincy to my face!

"I said look at me, Quincy!" Her black eyes impaled his.

He tried to look away. *This is just a nightmare! But why can't I wake up?*

"Hmm, not bad, pupils dilated and fixed," Celia said, her eyes stalking his. Her fingers wedged up his left eyelid then his right. "Perfect dose. Needless to say, I am the pancuronium bromide queen! Jersey used to say that, too! We experimented with it, you know, mixed it with other drugs, played with delivery methods—just to see what happens. Caused a few deaths on the street, but what can I say? That is the price addicts pay—sooner or later." Her self-possessed demeanor and grin, her voice control and intimidation were nastier than that of the Cheshire cat in *Alice in Wonderland.*

"Good news, honey!"

Honey? Now it's honey? What happened to Quincy?

"I learned a lot from all that experimenting, so you do not have to worry. Everything is going to be just fine—at least for a little while and that is where the bad news comes into play." She shrugged. "But like I say: not to worry. I am going to take real good care of both you and Beverly—and of course, me."

SEPTEMBER 17 – 11:00 A.M.

BEALE AND KEY RESIDENCES

Tires crushing shells punctured the morning stillness as the unmarked police car fishtailed into the Beale driveway. At the same time, the copper Viper was fishtailing into the Key driveway.

"Big surprise, the boy's truck is gone," grumbled Detective Rodney Clement, slamming on the brakes. As the car screeched to a stop inches from the rear bumper of Celia Beale's black Saab, his empty travel mug hurtled into the dashboard then plummeted to the floor in front of the passenger seat. He leered at the mug. "Sure could use coffee right about now."

His eyes shifted to the nondescript license plate on Celia Beale's black Saab. The twin to it—Pearle Key's black Saab—was still out there…"Somewhere."

Clement glanced next door. "At least the girl's VW is there. She's home—that's a relief in itself! Now to find the boy and the old biddy." He snagged the door handle and shouldered open the door.

As Clement hurled himself out of the driver seat, he heard Pomoroy hollering over and over again, "Bev! I'm sorry! Please open the door!"

Clement felt his hair stand on end. "Don't tell me the girl's not home!"

Leaving the car door open, Clement charged to the white archway then into the Celia Beale's tidy yard. *Crying shame what Doc just phoned me about. No kid deserves that, never mind two of 'em. Blast it all! I just don't get it; how could I have been so wrong about Hank Night? Why did the old bugger confess? Maybe Doc is right; I badgered Night too much. The bugger couldn't take it anymore, so he flat out 'fessed up. Shoot, there's got to be a happy ending in all this, but for the life of me, I wish I knew how to pull it off for those two kids—actually, all three of them.*

Clement put a fist to the Beale front door. "Chatham Police! Open up!"

He glanced at the cottage across the way.

"Come on, Bev!" hollered Pomoroy, double fisting on the kitchen door. "How many times do I have to say I'm sorry? Please, open the door!" Getting no response, he raced to the back deck.

Clement's ears started to ring. He chucked his pinky finger into one ear and rattled it. The ringing continued until he put two and two together—the ringing was coming from his cell phone. Uttering several undecipherable syllables, he yanked the phone out of his pocket then flipped it open.

"Detective Clement?"

"Yeah!"

"This is Luella Martin. I've been trying to reach Agent Pomoroy, but he's not answering. It goes right to voicemail."

"Pomoroy's tied up," snapped the detective, watching the young Fed, cell phone planted against one ear, barreling around the far front corner of the Key cottage. At every window, Pomoroy stopped, rapped on the glass, and peered in, one hand shielding his eyes. Every so often, he stopped and his finger jammed on the cell phone.

"Detective? Detective, are you there?"

"Yeah!"

Martin continued: "Preliminary examination of the three bodies indicates definite use of paralytic drugs. Lab

184

tests will either confirm or deny if the drugs used included pancuronium bromide. But we have a much bigger problem, Detective. Even if half of that missing paralytic was used on those three patients—and that's enough to kill six people! That leaves more than half of it unaccounted for! Just what is Cel... I mean, the thief intending to do with it?"

"I'm on it," said Clement, flipping the lid of his cell phone. He tried not to lose his cool, but those nasty red splotches were boiling up on his face again and sweat was making them itch to beat the band. "Where the heck is my team?"

Sliding the cell phone into his pocket, Clement felt his insides falling apart at the seams. His mouth was dry as a bone and yet sweat seeped from every pore. "Coffee," he grumbled as he pulled his handkerchief out of his back pocket. He swabbed the sweat off his brow. "Been up to our necks nailing that despicable dogfish, saving Pearle Key's reputation for the girl, and now it looks like we're not only going to have to save the boy, but we're going to have to save the girl as well." He stuffed the handkerchief into his pocket. "Just ain't right!. Gotta track them down ASAP!"

Sirens squalled in the distance, louder and louder. "Well, it's about time," Clement belched.

Scores of law enforcement vehicles, blue lights getting lost in the sunlight, came into view and then invaded the two properties. Hard-bodied men and women barreled out of the vehicles.

Clement gave a whistle, pointing as he commanded, "You three! Get this property swept and secured! Search out that old dogfi... Search out Celia Beale! And a male in his early twenties! Name's Quincy Beale! You three! Sweep and secure that property over there! Keep a lookout for the girl! Early twenties! Name is Beverly Key."

Just then, glass shattered.

Clement shot a look at the Key cottage. Pomoroy was reaching through the broken window of the kitchen door. The young Fed let himself in then moments later, exited the back of the cottage. He did a circle on the deck then leapt the railing and headed back to the kitchen door. He gaped at the broken glass then banged his hand on the side of the cottage.

Clement felt a jolt to his heart. "Pomoroy!" he hollered, charging to the gate of the picket fence. "Any idea where they can be?"

The young Fed spun around, jamming his hands into his hips. His head jerked side-to-side. "You think for one stinking second I'd be standing here if I did? Celia Beale finally slipped up, and here I am finger-picking my nose without a clue! To top it off, Bev's not answering her phone!"

"Pomoroy!"

The young Fed ran his hand through his hair. His face was stark as death. His breathing labored worse than a rider just finishing the Pan Mass Challenge in Provincetown. "Beale's been stealing drugs," he raved. "Fentanyl! Loads of it! Deadly crap! She's been one step ahead of me all the way in a cold-blooded cat and mouse game! And now she's on the run! I am so friggin' stupid! And now she's got Bev! She's got Bev! And Bev won't answer her phone!"

"Pomoroy!"

"I should've told Bev about the investigation," raved the young Fed. "We shouldn't have had that fight! If only I'd been here! She never would've gone with...with Celia Beale!"

"That old dogfish is the one who told Bev about the investigation?" Clement bellowed. "Why, that vicious two-spined... We've been set up!"

The young Fed groaned. "I can't believe I fell for it! And so did Bev!"

"The boy, too," Clement added. "Hook, line, and sinker! We all fell for it!" He grabbed the young Fed by the shoulders and shook him for all he was worth. "This is no time for head trips! Listen to me, Pomoroy! There isn't time!"

The Fed dropped his hands to his sides. His eyes zinged back and forth across the area like those of a wounded animal searching for a quick escape.

"Look, Pomoroy, I feel bad for you. The first lovers' quarrel is always excruciating. You're a grubby mess. But add circumstance such as this into the mix and...holy mackerel, that'll smack down the best of us! So, you gotta listen to me and listen to me right now! The girl's in danger! Danger, Pomoroy! The boy, too! And you and I are the ones who can track them down the fastest! Who knows how much lead that old dogfish has on us! So get your act together! Think this thing out. You know where the girl is! I know you know! Put the clues together! See her face in your mind's eye! Do it, Pomoroy! Do it now!"

The young Fed zeroed in on the top stair of the back deck.

"Confusion is giving way to clarity, Pomoroy. You see the girl sitting right there on that step, don't you, Pomoroy?"

"Bev," muttered the young Fed.

"Bev," echoed Clement, taking his hands off Pomoroy's shoulders. "Bev is sitting there. Bev looks terrified, doesn't she?"

"Bev is in bad trouble," said the young Fed. "Real bad trouble."

"And the boy," injected Clement. "Quincy. He's caught up in this, too."

Pomoroy eyeballed the place where Quincy always parked his pickup. Nearby, law enforcement was ripping apart Celia's car. "They had a real weird connection."

Clement broke out in a cold sweat. "Who's they?"

"Bev and Quincy," said Pomoroy. "Ever since they were kids they connected."

"Understandable," said Clement, circling his hand. "Keep it going, Pomoroy." His other hand reached into his pocked for a handkerchief then swabbed his face with it.

"Bev always knew beyond a doubt what Quincy was thinking; what he was feeling. She says he is a good guy, but Celia..."

Clement stuck the handkerchief into his pocket. "But Celia what?"

The color drained from Pomoroy's face. "Celia Beale is out to kill Bev and Quincy!"

Clement yanked his cell phone from his pocket. "I gotta issue an Amber Alert!"

"Pancuronium..." stammered Pomoroy.

Clement hit speed dial and waited. He shook the cell phone. "Come on! Come on! Pick up!"

Pomoroy snagged the detective's shirt. "We have to stop Celia Beale! There's no end to what she will do! There's no limit..."

Clement shook off the young Fed and put the cell phone to his ear again. "Get a grip, man!"

Pomoroy staggered backward, holding his head in his hands and moaning, "Get a grip.... Get a grip..."

The call was concise. It ended quickly. Then Clement flipped his cell phone shut and stuffed it into his pocket.

His gut told Clement to press the young Fed hard and don't delay one blessed second!

"Buckle down, Pomoroy, and tell me where you think Celia Beale took those kids. They had to have gone willingly, because that old dogfish is not physically strong enough to pull off a thing like this so quick. Nope, not if she had corpses on her hands."

The Fed's eyes popped open.

"What, Pomoroy? Tell me!"

"Beverly always says, 'Get a grip!' She says that she and Quincy say that all the time! I heard her say get a grip a million times!" The Fed eyeballed Beverly's red V.W. and then Celia's black Saab.

Clement egged on the young Fed. "They took the boy's pickup."

"They didn't take Celia Beale's car," Pomoroy muttered.

"No, they took the boy's pickup," Clement said again.

"The crunch of his tires is heavier than others," mumbled Pomoroy. "And the rumble of his engine is louder, too. Bev always knows when Quincy is coming or going. But it doesn't matter—she looks out at him anyway."

"The girl's down in the dumps about their imposed separation," prodded Clement.

"Yeah," said Pomoroy, squeezing his eyelids shut, concentrating. "They were real close as kids, she says. They had so much fun... Fun... Especially when Celia Beale and Pearle Key took the kids picnicking on Monomoy Island."

Clement planted his hand on Pomoroy's chest. "Monomoy Island? They have a boat?"

Pomoroy opened his eyes, his vision narrowing on the ocean at the rear of the two cottages.

"In all this time you never thought a boat?" Clement demanded. "You never thought about drug-runners stashing away high-speed boats?"

"I checked and double checked," said the young Fed.

"Aargh!" Clement exclaimed. "Now, that slimy dogfish has a boat at her disposal!"

"Bev never would have gone willingly to any other place than Monomoy Island," said Pomoroy. "And another thing: Pearle Key was hydrophobic. Bev told me so."

"I get it," said Clement. "Jersey Zayres or Celia Beale—maybe both—killed Pearle Key. While the dogfish was off working her normal shift, the drug pusher took the boat out and dumped the body at sea."

"The boat is at the Chatham Dock," said Pomoroy. "Don't know how I know that."

"You know," said Clement. "At this point, you know is all that matters."

Pomoroy hit speed dial on his cell phone then put the phone to his ear. "Still no answer."

Clement clamped onto Pomoroy's arm. "Let's go!" Breaking into a dead run, he let go of the young Fed and barked out commands, "Four black and blues stay here! Everybody else keep up with me!" Distant satisfaction reached Clement as he and Pomoroy raced neck and neck to the unmarked car. "Finally! A break in this godforsaken case!"

Tumbling into the driver's seat of the unmarked car, Clement chucked the key into the ignition and started the motor.

Pomoroy barreled into the front passenger seat.

They buckled their seatbelts in unison.

Clement spun the wheel, stomping on the gas.

The unmarked car did an about face, smoking up the driveway, tearing up the grass, and sideswiping the picket fence that separated the Key and Beale properties.

Pomoroy dug the fingernails of his left hand into the dashboard while his right hand clutched the handgrip above the door.

On the road, Clement glanced into the rearview mirror at law enforcement vehicles fishtailing out of the two driveways and folding into a single line behind his unmarked car.. Their spinning tires gave rise to cyclones of foul, black smoke that reminded Clement of Celia Beale's cheap perfume and henna-laden hair.

Summer And August

SEPTEMBER 17 – 11:30 A.M.

MONOMOY ISLAND

Quincy had no other choice than to stare at Celia, but he had the ability to think. *My own mother drugged me! I can't believe it! She drugged me to the gills with pancur...whatever it's called, and who knows what else! I can't move. I can't even talk! If only I could move my tongue. That nasty taste just won't quit! All I can do is sit here and look at her, listen to her mumbo jumbo. She is totally off her rocker!*

Her voice held a broken-glass edge. "I just cannot leave you two on your own, honey. You understand." She gritted her teeth, grinding them.

Get a grip! I'm a grown man! I can do whatever I want!

"No, you are *not* staying behind with that spoiled hussy," Celia seethed. "Over my dead body!"

Don't you dare call Beverly a hussy!

Celia rubbed her black leather belly pack. "It is such a shame that in this entire world not one single place exists where my baby boy and I can hide."

Hide? Hide from what? Quincy willed his mind to process her words. *What did I do wrong?*

"The world has gotten much too small, honey. Lots of eyes and ears—cameras everywhere. But as you can see, nobody's dogging us way out here."

Peripheral vision allowed Quincy to view the strand of beach that disappeared in the direction of Chatham. Not so much as one single seal bobbed its head above the brine. *Where did those seals go? What do those seals know that I don't?*

Celia grunted. "Take that Pomoroy. He is a Fed. Jersey told me so. Pomoroy thinks I am stupid—well, so did Jersey. I knew about Pomoroy that very first moment he stepped foot in the Rehab Center. I said to myself, 'Oh, yes, he is one of those Feds for sure.' Right away, he started nosing around. Everybody knows what he is up to now. And I know he knows Pearle and I have been pinching drugs and vending them to Jersey."

Ma and Aunt Pearle? Drug dealers?

"Pomoroy has no evidence," Celia said, "but it is only a matter of time before he does."

How can Ma just stand there like that? Hard as a rock! Wait a minute...does she have a gun in that belly pack? Can't see any bulges in her clothes.

Celia wallowed in deep thought. After a while, she sucked in a chest full of air and exhaled, "Now take that Jersey. Before he came along, I did my own dealing when times were tough, which was most of the time. I knew the moment Jersey took over the Chatham drug scene that he was one big slime-ball—more so than the idiot before him, which Jersey himself eliminated. He told me so. Then he says if I don't play ball with him, I will end up fish bait." Celia tossed a look at Quincy. "So, you see, honey, you did not have to tell me that Jersey is a jerk." She shook her finger at Quincy. "But you know, baby boy, you really have gotten too big for your britches!"

Baby boy? Britches?

She twisted up one side of her face and gazed out over the ocean. The hard edge softened. "But oh, how that man could sweet talk me when he wanted something. I actually thought Jersey and I were going to get hitched." Her entire face scrunched as she shook her head. "How stupid can I be?" Her voice overflowed with sharp self-disgust. "He strung me along—a long, long time." She shot a look at Quincy. "Didn't he, honey?"

For crying out loud, Ma! You know I can't talk! I can't even blink to let you know I'm listening! Look! Sweat is dripping off my eyelashes! It's trickling down my cheeks and neck and I can't do a thing about it! It's like I'm nailed to this stupid sand chair!

Celia rolled her head side to side. "Oh, how Pearle hated that man."

Didn't we all!

"You didn't know she caught Jersey boinking a sweet young thing at the Rehab Center, did you, honey? Well, Pearle confronted me about it the night before he..."

That's what that fight was all about over the picket fence! The jerk was screwing another nurse!

Celia seethed with contempt. "Talk about steaming mad! If Jersey was there, I would have killed the bum right there on the spot!"

Too bad you didn't, Ma!

"So then, Pearle says to me she thinks it is time we come clean about everything. Go to the cops? I don't think so! Well, you know, I almost killed *her* right on the spot."

Unbelievable! All this garbage going on and I was clueless!

"I tried to convince her that lifting drugs all those years from all the places we ever worked was the only way we got by, but no, she wasn't hearing anything of it, not one more minute of it."

I'm drooling! I can't even swallow back my own spit!

"Pearle was a weak, stupid woman. Always so completely dependent on me: how to act; how to dress; how to earn a living. If it weren't for me, she would be living in the ghetto on welfare. Truth is, honey, those weenie cottages of ours cost a fortune in taxes and upkeep—more bread than Pearle and I were paid, that's for sure. Add to that, bringing up you and Beverly... I certainly didn't think that one out, honey."

Beverly! Where are you, Beverly?

"You know I always took care of the bills and maintenance on both cottages. Pearle just handed over her checks to me. I gave her an allowance—just like a little kid! And she was happy as a clam! It isn't fair! *I* was the one who did all the worrying!"

Beverly! I know you're out there! Say something!

"That Pearle, she didn't have enough of her own motivation to fill a thimble. Well, now, I knew that we had to make sure you two had everything—without you having too much, you see. How would that look on a nurse's salary? But Pearle insisted we had to do the right thing. She kept squawking on and on about it, 'It's time! It's time!' I got so sick of her bellyaching!

Beverly! Your heart is racing as bad as mine! Come on, Beverly, answer me!

"Well, I knew I was not going to change her mind. So I says to her, 'Okay, let's come clean. First we have to tell Quincy and Beverly.'"

Tell us what?

SEPTEMBER 17 – 11:30

DETECTIVE CLEMENT'S UNMARKED CAR

"What's the plan, Pomoroy?" Clement asked as his thick hands strangled the steering wheel.

Traffic was light. A fair share of residents and fall tourists were in church and the rest hadn't hit the roads yet.

A green SUV, headed in the opposite direction, came up fast. "Hey, that's Curt!" shouted Pomoroy. His arm stretched in front of Clement and then his hand jammed on the horn.

"Hey, cut that out!" Clement blasted while jostling the young Fed out of the way.

The SUV zinged past as Pomoroy plopped back onto the passenger seat.

Clement banged his hand on the steering wheel. "Now you answer me! Right now, you cocky son of a so and so! Or so help me, I will take out my service revolver and shoot you!" He was seeing red, for sure, but he swore those nasty red splotches and Pomoroy were making everything a whole lot redder. "Tell me the plan!"

The young Fed leaned forward, craning his neck to see out the side-view mirror. "Curt's turning around."

"Pomoroy... I'm warning you..."

"I'm thinking, Rodney."

"Time for thinking is running out!"

"I know! I know!" Pomoroy shouted. His fists hammered the dashboard.

Clement drummed his fingers on the steering wheel. "Follow what you know is true in your soul, Pomoroy, because we are never going to surprise that insatiable dogfish. Monomoy Island is too big. Long strands of nothing but beach. She'll see us coming for miles, no matter what tack we take. Does that dogfish know how to pick her spot or what?"

Pomoroy hit speed dial on his cell phone, listened, and got no answer. "Celia Beale knows we will come. She knows *I* will come."

"She's got you hooked, Pomoroy, but don't let her reel you in." Clement glanced at the young Fed. "Don't you get it? When she sees you coming, she'll carry out her plan—whatever that is—and then she'll claim you harassed her. I can just see her now, spouting off, 'If that Fed had just left us alone, nobody would have died. Both of those kids would still be alive.' Public opinion is going to eat us alive."

Pomoroy winced. "Imagine the guilt trip I'll be saddled with?"

"No guilt trips allowed," Clement spat, dismissing the entire concept with a wave of a hand. "You and I *will* put a stop to her scheme! And that's that!"

Pomoroy shook his head as though dodging a swarm of flies. "Celia Beale is planning to survive all this."

"Yup," Clement said. "She is not doing this for the money. No way. It's the notoriety she's after. Can't put a price on fame. Yup, the dogfish is intending to survive. That way she can hype the story in the media. She is going for superstar status."

"What if we are wrong, Rodney? What if Celia Beale doesn't want to survive? Then what?"

"The old dogfish ends up a superstar no matter what," Clement grumbled.

"We outnumber her, Rodney."

"We got that, Pomoroy" Clement glanced at the young Fed. "Work the scenario, Pomoroy. Think it out loud."

"Goal: Hem Celia Beale in and save her victims," Pomoroy said. "Reality: Celia Beale can see boats, aircraft, and land vehicles."

"From miles out," Clement added.

"Don't panic, Bev," the young Fed murmured. "Worse thing we can do is panic."

"Don't get sidetracked, Pomoroy. The girl is not here. And it's high time you called her by the name she was born with."

"I'll be there real soon, Bev. Just don't panic."

Clement rolled his eyes. "Don't give in to it, Pomoroy. You're scared—more scared than you've ever been in your entire life. All because this time, you are head over heels in love with one of the victims. Cripes, I'm scared, too. I *like* the girl—and the boy. I feel real bad for him. Imagine living with that old dogfish all these years?"

"Then Celia Beale turns out not to be his birth mother," Pomoroy said.

"And his real name is August LaRosa," Clement said. "Well, not only do I not want any more bodies on my hands, I especially do not want the bodies of Summer and August LaRosa on my hands! Holy mackerel, what I'd do for coffee right about..."

"Clement! Watch out for those bikers!"

The detective snapped to, eyeballing the road ahead and the line of bikers dressed in red and black Lycra. He laid on the horn with his right hand as his left hand yanked the wheel into the oncoming lane. He saw their panicked eyes in the tiny rearview mirrors attached to their helmets that came to a point in the back.

A few of the bikers hit the soft shoulder. One mowed down a small plastic sign advertising hang-gliding lessons. A couple others rolled head-over-teakettle into a ditch.

Speeding past them, Clement muttered, "Sure am grateful I can't hear their curses." Worried about the potential of oncoming traffic, he accelerated and got around the last biker. As he pulled into his own lane, his heart was pounding his ribcage so hard it hurt. Hyperventilating, he reached for his handkerchief and swabbed his brow, cheeks, and neck.

The Chatham Inn and Conference Center loomed ahead.

Clement chucked the handkerchief back into his pocket. "Got anything, Pomoroy?"

"Dunes" the Fed said.

"Dunes run dead-center from one end to the other," Clement said. "Kind of like a backbone of dunes that changes all the time."

"Monomoy Island is a spit of sand, seven or eight miles long," said Pomoroy.

"Never would guess that in the 1800s a deep natural harbor existed out there," said Clement. "A sizeable fishing settlement used to exist there. A hurricane washed out the harbor, so everybody took off. No paved roads, electricity, nothing. Only the Point Light and lots of gray seals. Tourists take sightseeing planes and boats and such."

"How high are the dunes?"

"Fairly high," Clement said. "Not high enough to drown out a whirly bird thumping along the other side." He glanced at Pomoroy and noted the air of confidence that drove Clement nuts. This time, he was happy to see it. "Where are you going with this?"

"Pull over here!" Pomoroy barked.

Clement gawked at the entrance to the Chatham Inn. "Here?"

Pomoroy grabbed the door handle. "Pull over, Rodney!" His determined eyes were glued to the entrance. "Now!"

Clement yanked the wheel to the right and stomped on the brake. The unmarked car skidded to a stop. Tires screeched behind him. He braced for a direct hit—which didn't come—to his relief.

Pomoroy pulled on the door handle. "Keep your crew headed to the Chatham Dock and call me on my cell phone!"

"What are you doing? Pomoroy! Stop!"

The young Fed put his shoulder to the door. "Get hold of Debra Lawless, Rodney!"

"The *Chronicle* reporter?"

As the door swung open, Pomoroy hollered, "Tell her we have something concrete and to meet you at the dock! This is going to be her front row seat to the biggest story of her career!"

"Get back here, Pomoroy!"

Leaping out of the unmarked car, Pomoroy bellowed, "I got you now, Celia Beale!"

Summer And August

SEPTEMBER 17 – NOON

MONOMOY ISLAND

"So I managed to put off Pearle and the big discussion until the next night," said Celia, swabbing moisture off Quincy's face with a paper napkin—red and blue striped with white stars. "In the meantime, I call Jersey on his cell. He says he is out of town. What a liar."

Ma is living in the past! Quincy thought.

"Jersey is with that sweet young thing from the Rehab. I know because I hear her yapping in the background and I tell him so. Know what he says, honey? 'It's the TV!' Liar!"

She's shaking that napkin at Jersey—as if he's really standing there.

"And then that lying bum says Pearle is the one lying through her teeth! He never goes anywhere near the Rehab, he says, and I should know it's true, because if he went there, it will blow his whole drug operation to smithereens, especially with that Pomoroy hanging around there."

Bobby! By now, Bobby has to know Beverly well enough to know when something is wrong. Man, what I'd do for my cell phone!

"Pomoroy already knows Jersey is a dealer," Celia said, rubbing her black leather belly pack, "because he has been snooping all over the Cape." She shook her head. "What does he think I am, stupid?"

I'm taking the fifth on that one, Ma.

Celia shot a look at Quincy as if he had spoken out loud. For a moment there, he thought he had. For a moment there, he swore his heart stopped in the middle of a beat.

"But get this, honey! Jersey says he's going to make us official when he gets back to Chatham! He says he told Pearle all about it and she didn't like it one little bit. Well, I says, 'Too bad about her!' He laughs and then tells me to meet him the next day—at the Chatham Inn and Conference Center, no less!"

I've got to get to Beverly, thought Quincy. *She's close by, I just know she is.*

Get a grip!

He tried to get a whiff of the body mist Beverly always used, White Diamonds. *She has a thing for Elizabeth Taylor—and Leonardo DiCaprio. She has all their movies and watches them over and over when Pearle isn't...wasn't home.* Try as he may, Quincy just could not detect the slightest scent of White Diamonds. *Come to think about it, I didn't smell it on her this morning. Maybe she just didn't have time to put any on. We did leave earlier than other times.*

Celia paced in front of Quincy, her hands gripping her head. "'Jersey is going to make us official' kept going through my head. 'And he is going to wine and dine me at the Chatham Inn! Wow, fancy digs! What will I wear?'" She paused and smacked the side of her head. "What a chowder head I am!"

More than that, Ma. Quincy rolled his eyes. *Hey, I can roll my eyes! Now that's a step in the right direction!*

She continued to pace, her hands jouncing. "So I go and get all guzzied up in my favorite dress." She slid a look at Quincy. "You know the one, honey. The purple one with the plunging..." She put her hands to her bottom lip. "Oh! It isn't nice for me to talk like that around my precious little boy!"

She's looking at me the way she used to when I was a kid! When I wasn't supposed to hear something bad!

Her hand dropped from her mouth. "Oh, now look at you, honey. Sweating and drooling like that." She picked up another patriotic-colored napkin and squatted beside him. Dabbing his brow and cheeks, she gazed at him. Her head tilted to one side. "You are such a precious baby boy."

She actually believes I'm a drooly-mouth kid, again! Hold on... Beverly has to be drooling, too! Why isn't Ma wiping Beverly's face? She must have given her drugs, too. Maybe not the same kind as me... Oh no... Did Ma give Beverly something worse? Beverly! Are you okay?

Celia bolted to her feet, balling the napkin in her fist. She crushed it then tossed it away. A smile grew on her lips. "So, I look myself over in the mirror." She swiveled this way and that, examining herself in a mirror that wasn't there. "Not bad, if I do say so myself." She squinted at the invisible reflection and fingered her right earlobe and then her neck. "Just need a few bobbles. And perfume... Splash on lots of that perfume Jersey gave me. Oh, and my little cream-colored gloves and shoes! And clutch purse! Voila!"

Quincy didn't realize that he was tightening his brow. He was too distracted. *Look at her, strutting around like she's modeling that purple dress. What a nut job. Is she really going to trash me like she did that outfit? What if she trashed Beverly already? Oh, please, don't let it be true!*

Celia stopped in her tracks. Her brows fused as her hands clamped onto her hips. "Jersey says he has to meet that janitor at the loading dock out back of the Conference Center. 'Just sit tight,' he tells me. 'I will meet you in the parking lot when I'm done.' So, there I was, sitting in my car, waiting and waiting. Next thing I know, I hear shouting. That's Jersey! Who is he fighting with now? Better not be that sweet young thing from the Rehab. So, I get out of my car and sneak over to the loading dock. Well, there is that janitor, that Hank Night, and he is madder than a mud wasp in the fall! Cussing and fuming! Jersey is holding out for more bread for his special concoction. 'Things are tight,' hollers Jersey. 'That Fed nosing around everywhere is crimping my style, so the price is the price! Take it or leave it!' The janitor hollers back, 'I ain't forkin' over that much for one measly watered-down hit! I ain't got the coin!' Jersey shouts, 'Ain't ya picked up any treasures lately?' 'Nope,' says the janitor, 'nothin' for ya to take in trade, so *you* take it or leave it!' Well, I never seen Jersey so pissed off!" Celia straightened. "What is that?" She turned an ear to the sky. "A plane!"

Quincy listened. *A plane is coming! Well, it's about time, Bobby!*

Celia snorted. "It's just that idiot biplane dragging the ad banner."

Every fiber within Quincy railed. *No! It's got to be Bobby! Come and save Beverly! I don't care about me! Just save Beverly!*

The Piper Cub passed a hundred yards offshore, making one of several daily runs from the Municipal Airport. The banner trailing off the back was advertising sport fishing. As the plane banked to reverse itself and fly back on the other side of the dunes, Celia waved at it, carrying on the way tourists do. "The pilot is waving back at me, honey!"

Quincy felt like puking. *I can't believe this! If that pilot only knew what is going on down here...*

Quite pleased with her performance, Celia went on, "So, where was I? Oh, yeah. So, then, Jersey picks up the push broom and takes a swipe at the janitor. Of course, he misses. So the janitor high-tails it into the building, still cussing up a storm. I go up the loading dock and Jersey sees me. He puts down the broom and says, 'Oh, it's you,'—like I am nothing but beach trash! And the way he looks at me!

Just so awful! But I try real hard to ignore it. 'Jersey is having a bad day,' I tells myself, 'that's all.' You know how he gets sometimes, honey."

Quincy swallowed back drool, unaware that he was doing it. *Don't have to remind me about that jerk's temper!*

"Anyway, I ask him how it went with Pearle and he tells me not good, that he ended up breaking her neck or something like that and then he shot her up with fentanyl laced with heroin and cocaine and other stuff he scored on the street. His own special concoction. He so loves to brag, that Jersey. He says he just got back from dumping Pearle way offshore."

Without realizing it, Quincy tightened his fists. *Jersey did kill Aunt Pearle! Ma knew it all this time and didn't say a thing about it! Beverly has been going through hell and Ma just stood by and watched!*

Celia groaned. "I tell Jersey he shouldn't have done that, honey."

Quincy rolled his eyes and hooked his chin. *S-u-r-e. Bet the jerk felt really bad about that—not!*

She peered at Quincy "Well, you know how Jersey tricked Pearle, don't you?"

Quincy gritted his teeth. *It doesn't matter how he did it! Just let Beverly and me go!*

"Jersey took the boat up and docked it behind our cottage. Then he goes over and talks Pearle into taking a walk with him—so they can work out their differences, you see. Pearle never was too bright. And Jersey killed lots of people—he told me so. So taking care of Pearle was a piece of cake for him. Remember how he almost killed you, honey? When you were trying to get me to dump him? Jersey is a dangerous guy, honey, so better be careful."

For God's sake, Ma! That jerk has been dead for months! And let me tell you, I'm sure those drugs he pedaled killed a lot of people!

"Now that I think of it, honey, Jersey never did tell me where he ditched Pearle's Saab. I sure wouldn't mind having it. It always ran better than mine did. Not so many dings in the paint job either. I can sell mine—the cash will come in handy for your tuition, honey. Well, I guess none of that matters anymore. Know what? I bet dollars to donuts Jersey took Pearle's Saab to a chop shop."

Anger darkened her face; and it was the scariest Quincy had ever witnessed. Even horror stories infested with pointed teeth, weird colored contact lenses, and prosthetic makeup were nothing compared to her face at that moment. Fear consumed him. He smelled the fear reeking from every pore.

"Jersey says to me I better keep my yap shut," Celia seethed. "Or he will spill the beans to Pomoroy about Pearle and me stealing drugs from the Rehab. And he is going to say that I made him kill Pearle and that me and Pearle are sisters and..."

Sisters? Why didn't she tell me? I don't understand. What's the big deal about being sisters?

"Can you believe it, honey? Jersey actually threatens me that he is going to snitch to Pomoroy about you and Beverly! You know, about you two being twins and all!"

Twins? Beverly and I are twins?

Brother and sister? a voice in his head cried.

Who's my mother? Ma or Aunt Pearle? Come on, no way are Beverly and me twins. We don't even look like each other. On top of that, I've been in love with Beverly forever— and not like a brother. He felt as though an iron band was tightening around his chest, crushing his heart and soul. He closed his eyes, tight, and didn't realize he was doing it. *I can't love Beverly anymore—not like I do. She's my sister. But if she's dead, she'll never know about us. I won't even be able to love her like a sister.*

208

Celia rapped her fists against her temples. "I cannot believe it! I just stand there!"

Quincy's eyes shot open.

"What a rat that Jersey is! He looks at me in that real mean way of his, and you know what? He starts laughing at me! Right in my face! He says I look like fat whore in that purple dress! My favorite dress! And he says I must be the smelliest whore in Chatham! In all Cape Cod, for that matter! I tell him that smell was the perfume he gave me and he laughs in my face again. Well, I..." Her fingers dug into her temples. "I lost my mind! Next thing I know, that push broom is in my hand and I let him have it! With everything I got! Right on the noggin! Last time I saw that bum he was taking a nosedive right into that dumpster! Then I find out he landed on a metal spike!" She crossed her arms, gave a decisive nod, and stuck her nose in the air. "Good enough for him!"

She killed Jersey! The janitor didn't do it! She did!

Celia got to her feet. "Well, I run out of there like a chicken with its head cut off. I didn't come back to myself until...well...until I found myself sitting in my car in my very own driveway. It was pouring down rain, lightning and thundering like crazy. That is when I came to myself, honey. And then, of all the asinine things in this scummy world, that janitor ends up with Jersey's diamond ring, ear stud, drugs—all of Jersey's stuff! Imagine that, honey? All his stuff is right there in the cellar of that bookstore and I have no clue! Then that filthy janitor gets so wasted...his brain so fried that he actually confesses to killing Jersey! What a numskull!"

This is insane! Quincy thought, trying to get up. *I have to do something!* The sand chair creaked. He eyed Celia. Her teeth were grinding worse than fingernails on a chalkboard. *She didn't hear the creaking!*

"So then, honey, you go nuts over Beverly because of her taking a shine to Pomoroy. You say you are running away? Don't you know it is not right to separate twins? That is why, when I first saw you, and I wanted you so bad, I had to convince Pearle to take your baby sister, even though she didn't want to. No, twins cannot be separated!" Celia glared at Quincy, her hand rubbing her belly pack. "And now you have the nerve to tell that little hussy you are staying with her? Staying? Not going with me?"

She heard every word Beverly and I said!

She wasn't sleeping! cried the voice in his head. *She was faking it!*

"You have always been so irrational! So emotional! Hysterical!"

Hysterical? You're the one who's having a meltdown!

Suddenly, Celia slumped. "Oh, honey," she whined, her palms beckoning to him. "After everything I did for you? You are going to dump me?"

His entire body tightened, responding to his revulsion. *For crying out loud! I am not your boyfriend!*

"Don't you see? You leave me no choice?"

Choice?

She unzipped the belly pack.

What is she doing?

She took out a small, hard leather pouch.

Knowing the contents of that pouch strangled Quincy with fear. *She is actually going to kill me! Beverly, too! If she's not dead already!* He coughed, unable to get enough air into his lungs. *Beverly! Can you hear me? Please don't be dead!*

SEPTEMBER 17 – 12:30 P.M

MONOMOY ISLAND

Time, Quincy, Beverly thought as Celia Beale placed the small black leather pouch on his stomach. *Somehow, we need to buy some time. Time enough for the drugs she gave us to wear off. Time enough to fight her off until Bobby gets here. By now, Bobby has to know something is wrong. Thing is, will he come? After all those horrible things I said to him? I don't blame him if he doesn't come. But he* will *come! I just know he will! Then I will make everything up to him. I can face anything as long as I have Bobby—and you, Quincy, my twin brother—by my side.*

Celia Beale lifted the flap of the pouch and smiled with satisfaction.

Vials! Needles! Syringes! cried out a voice in the back of Beverly's head.

Terror raced through Beverly. *Quincy! You and I are in deep trouble!*

Celia Beale scanned the dunes and then the ocean all the way to Chatham. She arched backward into a vulgar stretch. "So, this is how it all went down, honey." She paused, a thoughtful look sheeting her face. "Oh, I forgot to... She tossed her hands into the air and took off for the boat. "Stay put, honey! I will be right back!"

Stay put?

Deep inside, Beverly sensed Quincy. *We have to stall until Bobby gets here.*

Try and move, whispered the far-off voice.

Beverly willed her body to move, but only random muscles obeyed. *I can barely move my fingertips.* Waves of hopelessness swamped her. *How are we ever going to fight off that witch if we can't move?*

Get a grip!

Beverly chastised herself. *Bobby* never *let me give up. Aargh! How wrong could I be? Talk about dumb! I'm so sorry about everything, Bobby. I shouldn't have gotten so mad at you. But when Celia said...*

Celia Beale strutted back from the boat and paraded in front of Quincy, her right hand braced on her hipbone. "Recognize this getup, honey?"

Beverly could not believe her eyes. *That's her purple dress! Complete with cream-colored shoes, gloves, and clutch purse!*

She wore that when we graduated from Chatham High School. I thought she was out of whack before, but she's totally bonkers now!

Celia Beale stopped and swung her body to the left and then to the right. "You don't know how glad I am that you cared enough to stash this gorgeous outfit behind those garbage barrels. If you didn't, I would have regretted not having it on this very special occasion." She hooked both hands on her hips, looking him square in the eyes. "You don't think I look like a fat whore, do you, honey?"

Beverly sensed his fury. *Get a grip, Quincy! We will get through this! We just need time!*

Celia Beale glanced over her shoulder at Beverly. Her dark eyebrows fused as her black eyes narrowed, skimming Beverly up and down, analyzing every breath.

A puff of wind sent the odor of cheap perfume in Beverly's direction. *Gross!*

She must have dumped the whole bottle on herself.

212

Beverly felt her stomach knot. For a moment she worried Celia might hear it gurgling. *When was the last time I ate?*

Should've eaten this morning, said the voice inside her head. *Those drugs would not have put us down so bad.*

Beverly's skin prickled. *I only took one gulp of that lemonade.*

Yecsh! What a rotten taste it left on... My tongue! I can move my tongue! Big deal...I can move my tongue.

No way am I going to magically jump up and fight off that witch.

Concentrate. No matter what, don't let her see anything! Don't want to get shot up with any more drugs.

She might do it anyway—just to be on the safe side.

Celia Beale blinked. Finally, she looked away.

Relief was so intense that Beverly thought she might throw up.

Celia Beale reached into her beige clutch purse and took out a cell phone.

She had her cell phone all along!

Celia Beale flipped open the lid, turned it on, and squinted at the dial. "It's getting late. Where are those suckers?"

She wants somebody to come and get us?

Celia Beale stuffed the cell phone into her purse. Then she took out another cell phone—a pink one.

Hey, that's mine! Beverly tried with all her might to get the words out, to jump up and rip her phone out of those filthy hands—to no avail.

Celia Beale flipped open the lid then activated the phone. Squinting at the dial, she pressed a key. "That Pomoroy sure is persistent!"

Bobby called?

Celia Beale grunted. "Come on, hot shot. Come and get your lady love."

Bobby will come! Just wait and see!
She is going to pay big time!

Celia Beale closed the lid on Beverly's cell phone and tossed it away. "Merle and I decided... Oh, you didn't know Pearle's real name is Merle, did you, honey? Well, mine is Delia."

Fake names, Beverly thought. She flexed her fingers and hands. *Hey, I can move!*

Celia Beale glanced over her shoulder at Quincy. "Get it, honey? Delia—Celia? Merle—Pearle?"

Clever.

Celia Beale looked skyward. "Hey up there. Let's be Delia and Merle from now on! What do you say? Celia and Pearle are history."

My left bicep is working! So is my left ankle!

I can purse my lips, Beverly thought.

Celia Beale hooked her hands on her hips and scanned the ocean. "So, Pearle—I mean Merle..." She looked skyward. "Sorry, Merle." She looked at the ocean again. "So, Merle and I get a day off at that hospital in Braintree. We decide to take the T into Boston to have a look around. It makes a stop in Brighton; and that is when this man and woman get on with the cutest little twins you ever saw. They have an older boy, too." Celia Beale slid a sidelong glance at Quincy. "His name slips my mind... But I don't care about him."

Beverly froze. *What if she goes after Quincy? I'm still too messed up to stop her.*

She might go after you.

Beverly feigned lethargy. *Do not react—not yet.*

"You know, Merle and I never did have kids," Celia Beale said. "We never even thought of marrying."

That close.

Celia Beale looked down at the sand. "We always wanted to have kids, though. Fact is, Merle is too much like our mother—mousy, you know—and I am too much like our hardnosed old man. He is so rotten to our mother— rotten to Merle and me, too."

Now we know where you get it.

"Mother ups and dies," said Celia Beale. "It dawns on me that if we two girls are ever to get out from under his filthy thumb, I have to be the one to do something about it. So I get him to drinking triple shots of bourbon. I light up cigarettes and put them in his mouth. I tell him, 'Our luck is about to change. I know ways to make our life better than ever. Trust me. I am a fast worker when things need to get done. That's a fact.'"

Beverly and Quincy gawked at each other.

"The booze sets in pretty good," Celia Beale said. "His taste buds must be real numb, by now. Real quick, I lace a shot of bourbon with two shots of antifreeze. It looks like the real thing. I give it to him and say, "Bottoms up! It is the only way to make sure the utmost of luck comes our way! Ready? One! Two! Three!" I light up another cigarette and stick it in his mouth. He takes a puny drag. I knock it out of his hand, making sure it lands in a pile of old newspapers."

It was all so easy for her.

"I lure him to his bedroom. He stumbles and gets to laughing in that drunken way of his. I help him along and when he flops on the bed, I light up another cigarette and give it to him. He passes out and drops it on the bed. I pry open his mouth and pour straight antifreeze down his throat. I rub his windpipe to make him swallow."

She's insane!

"The place goes up in a heartbeat. Whoosh! Merle and I barely make it out. Nobody asks us one single question. Not to us—two sweet young girls. 'Drinking and smoking in bed,' say the cops. 'Happens every time.' I never tell Merle what I did. I never tell anybody."

You just told us.

Celia Beale squatted and picked up a handful of sand. Grains sifted through her fingers as she rambled on, "So, here comes this pregnant woman with her husband and twins, the older kid, too. They sit a couple of rows in front of Merle and me. I can tell the woman is real tired. 'There is no other way we will ever have babies without a man,' I say to Merle." Celia Beale's features hardened. "Merle doesn't want anything to do with what I am thinking." Celia Beale snickered. "But I convince her."

Big surprise.

"'Neither of us has any use for men,' I tell her."

Until Jersey came along.

Celia Beale picked up another handful of sand and let it sift through her fingers. "I tell Merle we have to act like we don't know each other. Real careful like, we put our heads together, but I was the one who came up with the plan."

No kidding, Dick Tracy.

"I will charm that man and woman to death. Merle will do backup. Well, of course, I end up being hired as a nanny."

Was there any doubt?

She sure likes talking about herself. Just can't get enough. What an ego.

Celia Beale stood up and slapped sand particles off her hands. "A couple of times before that, Merle and I came down to Cape Cod and really took a shine to the place. So I get Merle to go down there and find two houses for sale. She hits pay dirt quicker than I expect. Two cottages right next to each other in Chatham—and they are far from just about everybody!"

Not like that anymore.

"But get this, honey. They are on Easy Street! Isn't that the funniest thing you ever heard?"

Oh, yeah.

"Merle buys one cottage for herself, cash—from pilfering drugs at places we worked. A couple days later, I come down and do the same for me. Merle pretends she used to have a husband in the military, but when he got assigned overseas, he met some floozy and did not come back. I pretend my husband took off with some sweet young thing and then they got in a car wreck in California and both of them died."

Of course.

Celia Beale trudged back to Quincy and sagged onto the sand chair to the left of him. She patted his shoulder. "I fell in love with my baby boy the moment I saw him."

Beverly panicked. *Stay still! Dead still!*

"Merle quits work at the hospital in Braintree and takes off for Chatham," Celia Beale said. "I go up to Brighton and do the nanny work, biding my time. Arrangements are made. Janice LaRosa is to go off to the hospital to have kid number four and I am to watch over the twins and the older boy."

Cheap perfume skunked up the air. Beverly fought off the instinct to gag.

Imagine what it's doing to me!

Elation zinged through Beverly. *Quincy! You rolled your eyes!*

Neck muscles are back.

Shake off those drugs!

Celia Beale removed her hand from Quincy's shoulder. Lacing the fingers of her hands behind her head, she flopped back on the sand chair, cradling her head. "But Merle keeps on moaning and groaning about giving the twins back to their parents. I cannot get it through her thick skull that we will never have our own babies and Janice LaRosa has four. I see no reason why we cannot have two of hers. She will never miss them. Besides, that woman and man will only make more babies. It will be so easy for them to replace the two we take. But no, Merle does not want anything to do with it. She doesn't want that baby girl. Never did."

Didn't want me? Mom...or Pearle...or Merle... Shoot, whoever that woman was!

"Year in and year out, all Merle wants is to give back the twins. She says they belong to Janice and Adam LaRosa. Nope, Merle does not want that baby girl at all."

She didn't want me? But she was always so good to me!

It doesn't make sense.
She loved me—I know she did!
How could she fake that all these years?

Celia Beale's voice had gotten so loud that she failed to perceive the distant rumble.

The twins almost missed it, too—but they didn't. *A motor boat! It's on the other side of the dunes! A helicopter, too!*

"Off Janice goes to give birth—and of course, Adam goes with her to hold her hand. I get the older boy all worked up about going off to visit his cousins in Stoneham. Off he goes. Bye-bye!"

If I only could stand up. Somehow, I'd find a way to make it to the top of that dune and flag them down.

"I bundle up the twins. Merle comes along. Fifteen minutes pass. There I am, calling the cops, raising a fuss and all. 'The twins were up in their cribs napping and I fell asleep on the couch!' I say. 'I never heard one blessed thing! Oh, those poor, poor twins! Oh, I am so, so sorry! It is all my fault!'"

The helicopter is going away!
Can't hear the boat!

Celia Beale was too wrapped up in fantasy to hear anything or to see that the drugs she had given Beverly and

Quincy were wearing off. "Those LaRosas are not about to pay wages plus room and board for nothing. I bow out, crying so bad. I stay at a rooming house in Quincy. Merle and I like Quincy—real nice place. Beverly is, too. Hey! What better names for our precious twins! Every day, I keep on telling everybody that I think I will go back to California, because that is where I am from and I got family out there and all."

Bold face lies!

"Things blow over. I take off. Everybody thinks I am on the way out to California. Instead, I scooch down to Cape Cod." Celia slid a sidelong gaze at Quincy. "And there you are, honey. My baby boy. Quincy. Waiting for his Ma."

I am going to puke.

"You are never going to be August LaRosa ever again," Celia boasted. "And Merle's little Beverly is never going to be Summer LaRosa."

We will always be Summer and August LaRosa!

"Merle loads up on henna and lightener," Celia Beale said. "She darkens her hair and Beverly's. She bleaches out yours, honey, but only that once, because…"

Celia Beale jumped to her feet. "Here comes that Fed!"

Bobby!

"Look at all those boats, honey!" Celia Beale exclaimed as her right index finger pointed in the direction of Chatham.

She isn't scared at all, Summer LaRosa thought.

August LaRosa nodded his head. *Not even a trace of fear in her voice.*

She is looking forward to this!

Celia Beale bubbled over, triumphant, "At last!" She fished a vial out of the hard leather pouch. "It is finally time, honey!"

No! Not yet! Summer LaRosa flailed her arms close to her sides the way seals flail their flippers. *Go away boats!*

Celia Beale removed the needle and syringe from the pouch. Her teeth made a horrendous grinding noise as she assembled the pieces then stuck the needle into the bottle.

More time! We need more time!

Celia Beale held the needle and bottle up high, watching the lethal cocktail fill the syringe. She pulled the needle out of the bottle then forced a small amount out of the syringe. Her voice was singsong, "Some for you, honey, and some for me." She stiffened her back and turned toward Summer LaRosa. Her brow tightened and her black eyes thinned to mere slits. "And some for sister dandy."

SEPTEMBER 17 – 1:30 P.M.

MONOMOY ISLAND

A blur swooped over the dune, happening so fast that at first, Summer and August LaRosa thought it was a fast moving cloud.

It's too colorful to be a cloud, Summer reasoned.

Much too colorful, August thought.

They strained to see the blur eclipsing the afternoon sun and then like a free-falling eagle, spiral earthward.

Celia Beale spotted it, too. "What in the world?"

Can't be a rainbow, Summer thought. *It hasn't rained in days.*

Through parched lips, August sputtered, "Hang glider..."

Summer squinted at the orange-suited and helmeted pilot. "Bobby!" she squeaked.

"It's that idiot Fed!" Celia Beale blasted as her hand shaded her eyes. "What are you doing up there? You are supposed to be on one of those boats!"

"Special Agent Robert Pomoroy coming in!" the young Fed hollered. "Celia Beale! You are under arrest!" Sunlight glistened off the barrel of the gun in his hand as he shifted in the harness and prepared for a sled run at the homicidal Celia Beale.

"Never thought I'd be this grateful to see that guy," August wheezed.

"Put your hands in the air, Celia Beale, and back away!" Pomoroy bellowed.

"In a pig's eye!" Celia Beale shrieked, stepping in between the twins.

Pomoroy aimed the gun. "Back off now, Celia Beale! Or I *will* shoot!"

"Go ahead!" Celia Beale taunted, putting her back to August and edging close to Summer. "You think you're such a great shot! Shoot! Are you that sure you will not hit your lady-love?"

"Get away from me, you stinking freak!" cried Summer, giving Celia Beale an ineffective shove.

"Shut up!" Celia spat, smacking Summer on the face.

"Stop!" August exploded. Summoning every speck of returning strength, he gnashed his teeth and flung himself at Celia Beale. His arms were like grapples clamping around her waist. She toppled backward. He closed his eyes and turned his head, preparing himself for impact. Her weight came down on him, crushing him. Air seemed to gush out of his every pore.

"Hang onto her, Augie!" Summer cried.

He sucked in air that reeked of cheap perfume and opened his eyes. Summer's big, beautiful, sapphire eyes were so close to his—and yet so far away.

Summer smiled a reassuring smile, the smallest of reassuring smiles, but a smile, no matter.

Determination swelled inside August, a volcano about to explode. He hung on for what seemed to be an eternity, the chair squawking under his and Celia Beale's weight. His arms began to cramp. N-o-o!" he raged. And then his strength evaporated.

Celia Beale shook off August LaRosa as if he were a mere water droplet on a dog's back. She swiveled around, her black eyes goring into him like ice picks. Her henna-black hair slopped forward as she seethed, "Oh, my sweet baby boy. Did you think for one minute, that you..."

A gunshot! It's echo zinged off the dune, running along the beach, and petering out over the ocean.

"That's a warning, Celia Beale!" Robert Pomoroy bellowed. "Put your hands in the air! Back away! Now!"

Hideous laughter exploded as Celia Beale arched her back. Her right hand came up, clutching the syringe. The point of the needle was aimed at August LaRosa! Right at his heart! And he could not raise one hand to protect himself from this maniac who up until a short while ago he called Ma.

Another gunshot! More echoes.

Celia Beale let out a stunned gasp. Blood seeped out of the corner of her mouth.

A third gunshot!

Blood rained down on August.

A loud crack—as loud as a lightning strike! The sand chair Summer was sitting in gave way. She hit the ground with a thud as the arm of the chair smacked into the pole of the umbrella. The umbrella tilted, putting a crimp in the pole. The umbrella broke away and the top half swung around like a turnstile, smacking into Summer LaRosa. The impact propelled her toward August and Celia Beale looming above him, needle in hand, bleeding like a stuck pig.

As Summer flopped against August, her flaccid right arm flew over him then her hand smacked into Celia Beale's lower arm. Instantly, Summer drilled her fingers into flesh and held fast. "Augie... help..."

Moisture filled his eyes. "I-I c-can't."

"Try..."

Once again, determination drove August LaRosa. He gnashed his teeth. *I can do this!* Straining, he willed—he commanded—every muscle fiber, *Shake off the drugs! Save Summer and me!* His heart raced, his breathing labored. His body seemed to be locked in slow motion. He pried his arm up. When it hovered exactly where he wanted it to, he let it drop. It landed beside Summer's—and like her fingers—his drilled into Celia Beale's arm.

"Turn her wrist!" Summer cried.

The twins strained. Somehow, managed to rotate Celia Beale's hand—and the syringe. The business end of the needle was now pointing up at Celia Beale.

A loud crunch!

The twins looked up. The hang glider had anchored on Celia Beale's back. Its weight—plus that of Robert Pomoroy—forced Celia Beale down upon Summer and August LaRosa. An ear-piercing shriek echoed throughout Monomoy Island as a rainbow of colors blanketed around all of them.

PRESENT DAY

CHATHAM

Any number of Chathamites—one in particular, the owner of Yellow Umbrella Books—staunchly maintain:

There are times when that god-awful shriek Celia Beale belched at the moment that needle impaled her evil heart reverberates throughout the dunes on Monomoy Island. When that happens, the odor of cheap perfume skunks up the air. And if the atmosphere is just so, that odiferous shriek makes it all the way to Main Street.

And so it goes that Celia Beale—alias Delia Something-or-other—is one of several discontented ghosts that haunt the cellar of Yellow Umbrella Books.

About K Spirito

K Spirito holds a Bachelor of Science Degree from Franklin Pierce College, class of 1998 and an Associate in Arts for Interpreting for the Deaf from L. A. Pierce College in California, 1982. In the '60s, she built power supplies for the Lunar Excursion Module that now sit on the moon. She transcribed Five Little Firemen by Margaret Wise Brown and Edith Thacher Hurd into Braille for the L. A. Public Library. She was a licensed Cosmetologist and owned a hair salon.

Born and raised in New England, K Spirito, always the history buff, loves to browse through microfilm of old newspapers. Noting articles of human-interest, she then weaves them into a variety of fiction—all set in New England.

K Spirito and her husband of over forty years, Sal, raised four children and are now, blessed with three granddaughters and five grandsons. K and Sal Spirito enjoy traveling, in-line skating, sailing, kayaking, and Mexican Train dominoes—and most of all, volunteering for the Franklin Pierce Alumni Association.

K and Sal Spirito are proud sponsors of Merrimack Youth Baseball. Among other organizations they support are the Franklin Pierce Alumni Association, the New Hampshire Association for the Blind, Concord TV, the Cape Cod Commercial Fisherman's Association, the Friends of Wrentham, the Granite Statesmen, Voices in Harmony, and the American Cancer Society. They are members of the New Hampshire Writers' Project (NHWP) and the Maine Writers and Publishers Alliance.

Other Books by K Spirito

FATHER SANDRO'S MONEY - *Historical Fiction*

The LaRosa family leaves Italy and lives through 30 years of real events spanning 1908 through 1930 in East Boston, New England and the world. - *Available on CD*

TIME HAS A WAY - *Inspirational Fiction*

Emma LaRosa loses her husband Seth after fifty-two years of marriage, and feels her life is over. She discovers Julie brutally beaten and life takes on new meaning. Mutual need creates a strong friendship and brighter futures for Emma and Julie.

YESTERDAY, TOMMY GRAY DROWNED - *Mystery*

Death doesn't trouble kids. If it does, they get over it quick. That's what the big people of Echo Lake, Massachusetts professed back in 1959. So what in God's name is Elizabeth Blair doing thirty years later, wandering a cemetery, looking for the grave of a fourth-grade classmate? Echo Lake spawns too many secrets—secrets that folks— including Elizabeth Blair— might just as soon abandon to the murky abyss that time leaves behind.

CANDY-COLORED CLOWN - *Action / Suspense*

Life is perfect for Julie Waters—great husband, gorgeous hundred-year-old brick manse perched upon a broad precipice overlooking the open Atlantic off Cohasset, Massachusetts, friends, family... Then she gets pregnant. Great husband, Ken, descends into a constant state of fretfulness, slugging down single malt Scotch and pacing about the manse that he and his first wife Regina restored just before the plane crash that took her and their only child Katrina.

- *Available on CD & Cassette!*

Spiderling - *Suspense /Thriller*

The White Mountains of New Hampshire is the setting for this Action Thriller! While attending Ecology Camp, Katrina Waters gets caught up in a terrorist sleeper cell. All she wants is her own identity and destiny—not the one her father wants for her and not the one terrorists intend for her. *- Available on CD*

PISCATAGUA - *Adventure /Romance*

Seventeen-year-old Chas Riley who is no taller than the average five year old seeks the love of Katrina Waters. Chas struggles with self-esteem issues, a heart condition, and the aftereffects of terrorism. Will Katrina view Chas as a real man? Or will she pursue tall, bronze-toned Bert Moro, an FBI mole who is never around when she needs him? This sequel to *Spiderling* is set in New Hampshire, Maine, and Massachusetts. *- Available on CD*

Works in Progress

Kathleen - *Fiction—Historical Journal*

You met Kathleen in **Father Sandro's Money**. You learn much more about Kathleen in **Summer And August**. Now you get to know the entire story of what happened after Armand was gunned down. Follow Kathleen and her two children on the path life leads them, through the intimacy of her journal.

Breinigsville, PA USA
22 March 2010

234627BV00001B/2/P